S0-FQW-789

Spritzerville,...Ohio?

By

Jason R. Koivu

Copyright © 2013 by Jason R. Koivu

All rights reserved.

ISBN 978-0-9910411-0-7

Published by C Street

Printed by 1984 Printing, Oakland, CA

Illustrations by Tommy Kovac

Acknowledgements

My deepest sympathies go to Marci Haneisen, who was tasked with editing this mess. Mess though it may have been, it was my mess and I was rather motherly about it. "My baby can do no wrong!" may have slipped out of my mouth once or twice. So criticizing my baby was Marci's thankless burden and she did a fine bit of yeoman's work. I have a great regard for editors. Their fresh eyes always find things you never even noticed were there. You all can thank Marci for this book being a much smoother read than it would've been. My many heartfelt thanks to you, Marci!

How about them illustrations, ey?! My god they're good! When my friend Tommy Kovac agreed to illustrate this book I damn near shit myself. I've admired his work for years and knew he'd do a superb job of capturing just what I was trying to get across. Tommy has produced many books of his own. You can, and should, find him online at www.tommykovac.com. Tommy, nobody does a better Poop Baby than you, baby! (It has corn for eyes, ha!)

My sincere thanks out to the following people, without whom this book would not have been made it to the printed page:

Matt Bornski, Craig Whitney, Dan Schwent, Sally Koivu, Marc Calvary, Mark Skelton, Angie Swanson-Kyriaco, Louann Lorden, Emily Kremer, Q (aka Eriq Christensen), Melanie Maher, Delaine Derry-Green, Daniel Koivu, Jason Murtagh, Frances Winkler, Kate Martyniouk, Devin Scott, Melodi Kownacki, Kris Koch, Luana Lopez, Dominique Rowland, Neil Saldana, Jose Rojo, Julie Kimball-Drake, Richard E. Koivu Jr., Bradley Bennett, Nadine Gomez, Lilo Huhle-Poelzl, Bonnie Kimball, Devon Bell-Turner, Dorothy Greeke, Kathleen Clark, Thomas E. Kovac, Susan August, Jeffrey August, Hilary Nagler, John Kimball, Leo Bray, Kyle Eckert, Cynthia McMeekin, Pauline Herr, Scott Roy, Kristine Oliveira, Anna Liza

Monti, Robert Donner, Brandie Sweetland, Jennifer Robinson Piersol, Danielle Butler, Katherine Gunther, Jasmin Brooks, Julie Fredericksen, Shanna Leslie, Ruel Gaviola, Androo Robinson, Emma Moon, Donna Stewart, Ron Hosler, Matt Schulze, Emi Umezawa, Amanda Winters, Lucy Pendl, Anthony Tedesco, Adam Stempel, Tessa VanDalsem, Warren Curry, Luis Falero and to all the others who shared their love and support!

And a special thanks to all the grandmas out there. How you doin'?

For Cherry
Without you no words would follow

Dedication page outtakes…

For Cherry
You're the best around! Nothing's gonna ever keep you down!

For Cherry
You are the wind beneath my wings…

For Cherry
Wanna get nekkid?

CONTENTS

Good day to you, sir or madam. Allow me to introduce myself. I am Bernard Wimple and although I haven't read the book you are holding, I believe it was written about me. It must be so, otherwise why would they have asked me to give you some personal details with which they might cobble together some sort of introduction? Well, it's not going to happen! You can put that right out of your mind! Oh surely I could tell you that I am the sole proprietor of Wimple's, a haberdashery in the lovely little town of Spritzerville; that I live alone with my pet toady because my family up and vanished one day; or I could tell you intimate details such as that I haven't quite found my one true love just yet.

However, I am a private man and these are all personal matters, so you'll not hear about the cozy cottage I live in with its small patch of overgrown greenery in the back, which I vow will have a proper garden in it one of these days. No sir!...or madam...or whatever thing might be reading this. I don't need anyone rooting around in my backyard, if you will, unearthing tales of my wayward and highly dependent brother licking lead paint off the bottom of rancid birdbaths, caressing other people's elbows, and generally having to be reminded to breathe. My level of annoyance with my own family is my own business!

So you can imagine I was a mite bit troubled when I learned a book was being published about me. I assure you, none of these stories were written by me. They were written down by something called a brianwig.

An exemplary example of the brain-picking brianwig

I am no man of science, but as I understand it, a brianwig is an insect the same size and shape of an earwig that crawls into your ear and wreaks havoc. Discovering I had one of these concerned me enough to do a bit of research on the matter, after I was done smacking myself in the ears that is. As it happens, brianwigs were meant to be called brainwigs, however, due to the common mistake people make of transposing the I and the A when writing either brain or Brian, coupled with the naturally poor spelling ability of scientists on the whole, the little beasty got stuck with the name brianwig. It also needed distinction from the common earwig, because earwigs do not necessarily crawl into your ear and start munching away, whereas brianwigs essentially do. That is to say - and this is the interesting part - they crawl on in when you're unawares, hang out in the brain area and feed off your past thoughts and experiences. Then it exits the ear, having caused no harm, except for a few recorded cases in which victims claimed to have felt "severely grossed out." After that it goes off and writes novels based on the stolen knowledge.

Disturbing? You're darn tootin'! I mean, that's plagiarism! Or so I imagined. I had a lawyer look into the matter and apparently a person's thoughts only become their intellectual property when they write them down and sign their name to them. Since I am a salesman, not a novelist, that's unlikely to happen, so I took another tack: I gave in and, to a certain degree, embraced the situation. After all, it's not every day one has an autobiography written about them by someone else. And honestly, there was really no other choice. I may not be happy about it, but I've been assured that although he's a bit prosy and adds his own flourishes now and then, my particular brianwig - this Koivu fellow - while no Shakespeare, could be worse. At least he's not in and out of my ear incessantly like that brianwig by the name of Stephen King. No, Koivu pops in, takes a few notes and then goes back to his squalid little abode to whip up some cracking good tales, so I imagine. All the same, don't believe everything you read! I'm sure there's some terrible lies about me herein. Writers will be writers, so you must allow for poetic license…hmmm. Does anyone know where they obtain those licenses? And can they be revoked at all?

An exemplary example of a Bernard Wimple

2

Helping Knobby Get Back on His Feet

On his weekly stroll along the fairly bare yet modest hills overlooking Spritzerville, the terribly quaint village where he lived and worked, Bernard "Beanie" Wimple crested Topham Hill and stopped to rest on a soft and fleshy lumpopotamus that, like him, was in no rush to get anywhere anytime soon. When younger, Bernard ruled his days from morning until night, but now in his middle years (or at least what he hoped were his middle years) he spent his days as idly or industriously as the day ruled. If a busy day arose, he rose to meet it and if a lazy day loped up, he lazed along with it. It's not that he wasn't industrious, he just wasn't as enterprising as he once was. If he was being completely honest, he'd tell you that with each passing day he felt as if he'd rather be doing a little bit less than the day before.

"Monday is an excellent day for doing a little bit less," said Bernard aloud to no one in particular as he reflected on the sun's brilliant illumination of a single cloud and added, "and a marvelous day for a ramble. Much better than going to work." He considered the sense Kaiser Moose O'Weeny, the local ruler of all the things, had in enacting a law that gave everyone Mondays off. It was undoubtedly the most popular law the unpopular Kaiser had ever passed, Mondays being the most hated of all workdays. Of course it meant having to work on Saturdays in exchange, but Bernard believed as did the greater majority of the people, that one must make concessions now and then if one wanted to better one's life.

Taking his tweed duckbill cap from his perfectly round head, he laid it on his perfectly round belly and let the wind whip straight the one wave in his stringy hair. His small, smiling eyes wandered down the slope following the Tumbler as the stream bubbled this way and that around pink heather bushes and clusters of ferns, over smooth rocks and shiny pebbles, through all sorts of ankle-tangling vines and knee-high shrubbery right down into the village. From here he could just make out the rooftop of his haberdashery amongst the shops on Main Street.

"A dog would be nice," he said, regretting his choice of pets at a time when a longer-legged companion would be such good company. It's not that he wasn't fond of the pet he had, but his beloved Gaiety couldn't manage such long walks. Its stubby little legs were better suited for a light crawl about the living room or perhaps the occasional hop, if the toady-like creature felt up to it. Imagining its shiny, brown nose and big, watery eyes that pleaded for acceptance, Bernard felt bad for thinking poorly of his pet toady, who seemed to live for the sole purpose of giving pleasure by boosting its owner's ego. It flattered him profusely and made him feel better on especially bad days. The day before yesterday had been an especially bad day at the end of a long, wearisome week in which all Bernard had to show for sales was a feather his upstairs tenant, Mr. Myles Thyghmaster, bought for his fez. *Bernard would agree with you if you too thought it strange to want a feather for a fez.* When he got home that night, Gaiety had complimented Bernard on his handsome, brown eyes. As always, it was apropos of nothing, but a nice thing to say nonetheless.

"They're not the worst set of eyes I've ever seen," Bernard said and he wasn't being immodest. They were one of the few things about him that had any chance of standing out in a crowd, shining like a couple of highly polished jasper marbles as they did. Other than that, Bernard was a garden-variety sort of fellow from his looks to his middling athletic prowess. The opinion of those who knew him best was that - while not being an ugly sluggard without an ounce of gray matter who passed his days knocking down perfectly good fence posts with his forehead and then frightening the old and young with the results - he was by no means a dashing Greek god who kept his mind busy with a bit of calculus during an afternoon's brain surgery. A little shorter than tall, slightly fatter than thin, neither a brilliant brain nor a hopelessly bumbling buffoon, he simply hovered around average. That's not to say there weren't ways in which he was above average. For instance, take his midsection, it was becoming more and more above average with each passing year. There were a few other areas in which he was decidedly below average, but we won't mention those, because it's not polite.

Bernard's fingers jingled the two coins from that lone sale still sitting in his pocket, while the fingers from his other hand smoothed out his twirly moustache, all the while fingerlessly admiring the Kaiser's windmill across the valley over on top of Best Hill. His lingering eye spotted someone, no more than a speck of a figure at this distance, crawling up the slope towards it. A squinting inspection rocketed Bernard's mood up from contented to delighted as he recognized the bent form of his old chum Reginald Dillon Fitzgerald. At school he was called either "Fitzgherkin" or "Knobby." Neither nickname was very nice, but as is the case, the way words are said can make all the difference. The meaner kids spat "Hey Fitzgherkin!" at him, while his friends called out "Good ol' Knobby!" with welcoming smiles and jovial pats on the back whenever they saw him. He was great fun, well liked, and Bernard's particular friend ever since they won second prize together for a science fair project in which Knobby used Bernard's head, bald and covered in baking soda, as a decent facsimile of the moon. That effort proved more success than their originally intended electricity project in which they rubbed so many balloons on Bernard's head that most of his wispy hair fell out. But these days Knobby lived in Weezy and though it wasn't far, the two friends didn't get to see one another as frequently as they might like, a common occurrence when folks leave school and leap (or lurch) into the "real world."

Trudging up the hill with his head down, Knobby appeared to be hiking with a purpose or perhaps something important on his mind. Bernard hailed him from across the valley with a big wave and a, "Hoo! Hoo! Haloooo!" but to no avail. His voice wouldn't carry. So, with a yank of his hat, he headed as straight as he could for the windmill, skirting a patch of thorny woonbrush on the way down and picking a careful path through the Sumpkin Moss Mire in the valley below.

Halfway up Best Hill he popped out from behind a blueberry bush and accidentally panicked a flock of sheep that went stiff-legged and collapsed in paralyzed fright at his sudden appearance. The paralysis was a harmless and temporary condition, and in no way did it hinder his hooting at the cottony puffs with legs as they toppled over into the cushy grass as if falling from stilts. What cut the very heart out of his hooting was an eerie moaning that slithered over the hill, whirled around him and blew ice into his pores.

"Just some no account ghost doing its darnedest to spook the bejeezus out of whoever or whatever might be within earshot. Well, if that is its intent, it's doing a damn fine job of it," said Bernard to himself, his vocal cords having slipped into his shoes. Armed with less than a full respect for the often shiftless spirits that inhabited these hills and a longing to see his friend, he forced his feet to move again. Each slow step forward was followed by a hesitant pause as he held his breath and listened. There it was again! The ghoulish groan set the fingernails of his right hand against the skin of his left. He tried not to think about the worrying feeling in his bowels as he peeked over the final bush between him and whatever was making that scarifying noise. Before him at the top of the hill was the windmill and nothing but the windmill, or so he thought.

"OOooooOOooohhhhh," the phantasmic voice moaned, drawing Bernard's eyes, shaking in their sockets, to the base of the windmill. Lying there prostrate in the grass was the motionless body of his friend. "Whoosh! Whoosh!" went the massive swinging blades of the windmill, spinning dangerously close to Knobby's noggin.

5

"Knobby!" cried Bernard, bounding over the bush and sprinting the rest of the way up the hill until he knelt by his friend's side in the thick grass. Knobby's green hue shown more olive than his usual cucumber. Bernard dragged him away from the whirling blades and shook him gently until his eyes flickered open. "I thought you'd been done in. What happened?"

"What happened?" asked Knobby in grave earnest, his worried eyes seeking answers with desperation before latching on to Bernard's face. "Beanie?"

"It's me, my old friend. It's me," said Bernard fighting a tremor in his voice as he attempted to hold a steady resolve against an unexpected upwelling of emotion at the sight of his injured and frightened friend. He turned his head up and away to keep the condensation in his eyes from condensing too much and turning into tears that might roll down his cheeks and betray him as the old softy he was. It was a trick he'd employed throughout his life and unfortunately it gave him the appearance of being aloof and uncaring, an undeserved reputation held of him by some.

"What are you doing here? And where is here?" Knobby still wasn't completely himself, though his color was coming back.

"Where is here?" repeated Bernard, questioning his friend's question.

"*Where is here?*" Knobby questioned his friend's questioning of the question and then he grimaced and rubbed his head. "What kind of a question is that?" The clouds that had covered his eyes cleared away and a full recollection of where he was and what had happened woke him like an alarm clock. "We've got to get out of here!" he shouted, using Bernard's arm, shoulder and head as leverage in his mad scramble to get to his feet.

"Why?"

"*Why?* Look at the Kaiser's windmill. It's broken." Seeing the confusion all over Bernard's face he explained, "I broke it with my head." He flipped back his curly locks, revealing a nasty bump on his forehead that was almost as big as the ones that covered his whole body and gave him his nickname. Bernard leaned back for another look at the windmill. One of the spindly stocks that its sails rode upon had indeed cracked. Though Knobby couldn't recall it for the time being, what had actually happened was that he'd absentmindedly walked right under the windmill. One of the stocks grabbed him by the collar of his grease-stained shirt, lifted him up and then snapped at its apex, dropping him on his head and causing the extra bump, as well as his forgetfulness and inadvertent distortion of the facts.

6

"Why'd you break it?"

"*Why'd I...?!*" Knobby looked absolutely punched-on-the-nose hurt. "Oh Beanie, how could you think I would do such a thing?"

"But you just said you did."

"You're hearing's gone wonky, my friend! No, no, no. I was just walking along minding my business and it hit me!"

Bernard knew that when Knobby said he was "minding his business" what he meant was he had been thinking about the catering business he'd been trying to get off the ground recently. Knobby was an excellent cook, but terrible with money. It was very likely he was deep in thought on this matter with his head down as usual, not watching where he was going, also as usual.

As Bernard steadied his wobbly-legged friend and brushed the grass from his napkin trousers, he noticed Knobby's money purse on the ground upside down and open. He picked it up and seeing there was nothing in it, started looking around for coins.

"You won't find a penny. I'm skint, my friend, bone dry. Now come on! We don't want to dally around here!" And with that, Knobby took off down the hill in the direction from which he came. With legs not half as long as his friend's, Bernard struggled to keep pace.

"But shouldn't you go explain what happened to the Kaiser?"

"And have him fricassee me?" hollered Knobby over his shoulder. "No thank you!"

"He'd never do such a thing."

"He certainly would if he found out it was me who'd broken it. Besides, I can't afford to pay the damages to get it fixed."

"If you don't go and he finds out it was you, that'll only make it worse, won't it?"

Knobby slowed and eventually stopped to ponder this while rubbing the hairy knob at the end of his chin. Bernard could see he'd gotten through to his friend at last and raced to produce arguments that would back up his point, not out of any egotistical desire to be right and certainly not because he wanted to see his friend suffer, but because he didn't want to see his friend become an outlaw. A mere whiff of an idea came to him, which he immediately snatched up and served to Knobby, perhaps a tad too quickly. Like taking a cake from the oven too soon, ideas should be cooked all the way through, too.

"You know, the Kaiser's spies are everywhere." It was only a rumor and one Bernard didn't truly believe, but by the sharp rising of Knobby's caterpillary eyebrows, it was clear he did.

7

"You're right," he said with concern. "Someone could be watching us right now even. That's decided it!" It seemed doubtful to Bernard as he looked around the hillside, treeless from here to the top with nothing to be heard but the almost inaudible murmurs of a cluster of grumbling grasswhackers. Certainly grasswhackers could be spies, but these appeared to be of the common variety and rather unlikely to speak to anyone other than their own kind. Still, if the idea motivated his friend to do the right thing, Bernard was glad it had worked.

In fact, he went on extolling the virtues of honesty, of being forthright and owning up to one's mistakes as they trekked along the rounded ridge, over the next verdant hill and down into the valley beyond on their way to the Kaiser's castle. Knobby listened politely, nodding as if he agreed with Bernard's moralizing, but what really concerned him was the possibility of being caught. If admitting his guilt now would lighten the sentence he'd receive rather than if the Kaiser should find out what had happened from his spies, then he was all for taking the moral high road.

While traversing the stagnant and rancid Rush Waters, one of the many treacherous stink swamps found in these parts, Bernard began to second-guess himself. By talking Knobby into this, he thought as he dodged to avoid another soggy burp, he was getting his friend into trouble that might never have found him in the first place. Plus, the Kaiser could afford to have the windmill mended. It was a minor breakage at best. Besides all that, this walk was becoming entirely too long.

"Perhaps I'm meddling," he began mumbling aloud, a habit he'd developed from spending so much time alone lately. Knobby slowed up to walk side by side for the brief period the path allowed. He clapped Bernard on the back, beaming a benevolent smile down on him.

"O'Weeny would've certainly slapped me with a fierce fine. I can't afford that, never mind paying for the repairs. You've saved me no small amount of coin, my friend!" Bernard could see that his arguments had been all too persuasive and he regretted sitting in on that debating club contest back in school that one time. It clearly had had a bad effect, evidenced in the fact that he was out here in this miserable swamp when he could be at home enjoying a crumble of week old bread in a saucer of pale tea, his only culinary extravagance in these days when his finances were not what he'd wish them to be. But that's the way of things. If you're going to put your bum on the line for a friend, you have to expect it'll get nibbled now and again.

As it happened, bum nibbling was an immediate concern, being that they were passing through low, foggy bog lands within sight of a red beck fox, one of those rabid and guileless beasts eager to make a meal of your buttocks, the dish they most relish. It sat on its haunches in a clump of cat-o-nine tails on a tiny island with enough water between it and them to make the swim more trouble than the meal was worth. Whatever the level of danger, Bernard was glad to put space between it and them. Fully forgetting about the fox would feel even better, so he stuck up a conversation.

"Why were you so worried about going to see the Kaiser in the first place?"

Knobby hesitated, looked embarrassed, but went on.

"Do you remember the garden party thrown at the castle last season?" Bernard only remembered hearing about the party. He hadn't attended, feeling it wasn't a good enough reason to close down his shop for even one day, even if on that particular day everyone from miles around was going to be at the party and not in the village buying hats at shops. "Oh forgive me Beanie, I forgot you had to work that day. Well, all you missed was His Majesty's Imperial Highness throwing a fit all because someone debauched Malady's Crumpet before he had the first go."

"You?"

"Right there in the middle of the party for all to see. Couldn't help myself! Can you blame me, I mean, who doesn't love a tasty bit of crumpet?"

"I admit," admitted Bernard, "I've been guilty, in younger days mind you, of having a crumpet or two in my bed--"

"I like to poke mine," said an excited Knobby while making the repeated motion of poking his finger into his balled up fist, "and fill it with cream!"

"But Knobby, Malady's? And at His Majesty's Imperial Highness garden party in front of everyone?"

"I know! I know…but you can hardly blame a chef for his momentary loss of control around tempting desserts."

"Was it worth it?"

"It was the best I've ever had!" Knobby's eyes lit up with dazzling radiance, then glazed over as if he was seeing a magical fireworks display from a loop-crazy rollercoaster on the Moon.

Reginald Dillon Fitzgerald was a good chap with the best intentions, but he had a habit of getting carried away and finding himself in jams, and they were not always the sweet, spreadable kind either. Such had been the case at this party. You see, Malady's Crumpet, a cherry juice-infused griddlecake, is the prized dessert at feasts in these parts, as well as

9

parts unknown. It is the *"festin de delices final"* as His Majesty's Imperial Highness the Kaiser liked to call it. As host, he also claimed "first bite" privileges, meaning his crumpet was not to be sullied by the caprices of other men until he'd had his fill. Knobby was sensible in some ways, but when he lost his head it was most often over a delectable dessert. He had done just that and at the Kaiser's party, an affront not likely forgotten by the high and mighty man.

"I'm sure O'Weeny's forgotten all about it," reassured Bernard.

"Maybe you're right, but even so, he won't be pleased about me breaking his windmill!"

"We'll just explain it was an accident and tell him you'll pay for the damages as soon as you can. I'm sure he'll understand." But Bernard wasn't sure he'd understand. From what he heard, the Kaiser was a quick-tempered, grudge-holder. Still, one had to have hope and Knobby looked like he could use a little of the stuff.

A couple cups of hope and two pints of courage would've done both of them good when they emerged from Stone Forest, a forest of stones. Before them, atop a craggy rock, sat the grouchy-looking Castle Mucusplug. The proud O'Weeny family claimed the name was of Narbonese origin meaning "wealth of bovine god splodge" and insisted it be pronounced "moo-coo-sploo," but nobody was fooled. It's mucus plug.

Truly a terrible place for a garden party

The cold, gray stone that made up the castle walls and towers dug into the ground as if clinging to the rock so that it could lean out over the edge and, with prejudice and disapproval, glare down through its thin, slit windows at those who dared approach.

"There was a garden party held here?" asked an astonished Bernard, seeing the castle for the first time and wondering how pleasant a garden party it could possibly have been up there amongst the jagged rocks atop the flowerless, barren peak.

"A tad dreary, isn't it?" said Knobby as he led them to a narrow, zigzagging set of stairs cut into the rock's surface. Bernard all but rode Knobby's rump up the precarious path as the two began the arduous climb.

Upon reaching the top, red-faced and puffing hard, they stood with hands on hips at an ugly, iron-barred gate pressing an annoying door buzzer for what seemed like ages until they were finally granted entrance by a relatively chipper 103-year-old yak herder from the Zavkhan province of western Mongolia. His fuzzy three-piece monkey suit and gap-toothed grin, masking his inability to understand a word they said, lulled Bernard and Knobby into thinking that perhaps this would turn out better than they expected.

There is a saying, "two shakes of a lamb's tail," which means a short period of time. It seemed like that lamb only had time to shake his thing once before Bernard and Knobby were positively flying back down the stairs and away from the castle as fast as they could. Their meeting with the Kaiser had not gone well. He'd become enraged, stamping his feet, snorting and bellowing, all the while demanding the windmill be fixed immediately out of Knobby's pocket. And yes, he did remember Knobby and insisted his crumpet's virtue be restored. Knobby only exasperated the man further by asking the reasonable question, "What does that even mean?" which sent the pint-sized dictator soaring to searing heights of indignation and fist-balling fury. In fact, at that very moment he was in the castle's highest tower shaking his fist menacingly while casting unmentionable cussings down upon them and barking commands to his minions.

"Did he just say 'Release the clowns!'?" asked Bernard between breaths.

"I tell you, your hearing is not what it once was, my friend! Clearly he must've said 'hounds'."

The air erupted in barking howls and vicious snarling. The ground trembled with the thunderous thumps of dozens of heavy feet chasing after them down the steps. The idea of being torn to shreds by a pack of vicious dogs shook their amygdalas and held their intercalated neurons hostage, which a neurologist will tell you, frees up your feelings of fear and allows them to do their worst.

"Don't look!" shouted Knobby who was looking over his shoulder, but it was too late. Bernard's curiosity smacked aside his restraint and he glanced over his own shoulder.

11

"CLOWNS!!!" he screamed. He wished he hadn't screamed. It wasn't a very manly thing to do, but he couldn't help himself. The horrific sight of a horde of hideous clowns gaining fast upon them terrified him. The beastly creatures broke out in hysterical laughter from hugely distorted mouths, though a few just silently grinned while others blared away on their ear-piercing party noise-makers. Rolling and staring from their sockets, their eyes flashed wild, bloodshot and unblinking, except for the one named Blinky. They wore smeared-on, garish make-up like demon jezebels, but to be fair, their colorful outfits were quite festive and not scary in the least. Some wore silver bowties that spun like sharp, steel propeller blades. Perhaps they may have only been ornamental and plastic, but Knobby and Bernard weren't about to stop and ask. They were too busy fleeing for their lives with worse things to worry about as they dashed down the stairs, taking them two at a time when they could and occasionally coming very close to falling off the edge due to the lack of a hand railing, a flagrant safety code violation. Even so, the clowns couldn't catch them. Realizing this, they opened fire upon the pair, squirting powerful blasts of water from fake flowers stuck in their lapels. The wet jets whizzed by Bernard's ears and elbows. Knobby took a direct hit to the back of the head, throwing him into a somersault that nearly knocked him off the ledge a hundred feet from the ground below. Bernard helped him to his feet and the two friends scuttled off with water splashing all around, soaking the stairs ahead of them and making the stones slick. They had to slow down or risk falling off the edge, but that brought the enormous clown shoes flapping upon their heels, and the closer they got the more they taunted with giggles and chortles, malevolent in their jollity.

"I don't think we're going to make it!" cried Knobby over his shoulder.

"Just keep going!" huffed Bernard. "I don't cherish the thought of being torn to shreds and devoured by a pack of clowns!"

It was a wonder they weren't eventually taken down by the water blasts and slippery stones. However, the stairway often wound back and forth on itself, so that their zigzagging movement made aiming difficult for the clowns, whose ridiculously oversized shoes, so unwieldy on the stairs, kept the two friends just out of their clutches. By the time Bernard and Knobby reached the bottom they were all but tripping down the last few steps. Fairing even worse, the clowns toppled almost on top of them, falling into a colorful, disheveled pile.

"Don't look back!" Bernard listened to Knobby this time and ran, face forward, as fast as his short legs would carry him into Stone Forest just behind his friend. Like fat fingers as tall as trees, the dark, oblong stones surrounded Bernard and Knobby as they wove in and around them, going deeper and deeper into the forest, hoping to lose themselves amongst the stones and praying the clowns didn't track as well as hounds. Though the threatening growls and freakish laughter echoed all around, it was the clowns' heavy feet pounding the ground that they could hear and feel the most. Gaping holes scattered every few feet through out the forest floor made the going a good deal more hazardous. Twisted ankles were hardly worth worrying about compared with the injuries befalling anyone who'd be falling into one of these pits.

Knobby picked up a rock and hurled it off to one side.

"What'd you do that for?" asked Bernard. Knobby shushed him. The rock struck one of the standing stones, barely audible some distance off. *Thump! Thump! Thump!* Heavy footfalls faded away towards the click of the rock on stone.

The friends took off at a sprint again, running until Bernard's heart and lungs pumped like the churning bellows of a flaming forge. It wasn't long before he had to stop, bent double and gasping for air as he begged Knobby to go on while he still had the energy.

"Nonsense," said the lanky and fit Knobby, barely winded at all. He stood by his friend with a hand on his shoulder and listened with an upturned ear. Echoes of manic laughter and the flapping of shoes bounced off the high standing stones. Far away they heard an ominous honk, then another off to the left. It happened again. The honking increased and developed into a steady pattern that crept ever closer.

"Oh no!" whispered Bernard. "You don't think?"

"I'm afraid so," answered Knobby, "they're communicating back and forth by honks."

"They'll track us down for sure!" said Bernard, worry edging his words. The acoustics amongst the stones were unreliable, throwing the sound about and making it appear the clowns were all around them, ready to burst out from behind the nearest boulder. The very real possibility that they might do so made Bernard extremely jittery. He clenched his bottom against an intense urge to go number two. Knobby, peering out from behind a stone and listening as hard as he could, spun around and grabbed Bernard by the sleeve, tugging him along as he sped off again. There was no time for Bernard to even think about finding proper bathroom facilities.

As they ran they came upon an enormously wide boulder. Following closely on the heels of his longer-legged friend, Bernard misjudged which way Knobby was going to go, and the two separated as

13

they went around the massive stone. Once out of sight of his friend, Bernard felt a fleeting sense of panic that made his legs go all stumpy. He waddled on, assuming he'd circle around and reunite with Knobby on the other side. That was not quite what happened.

When Bernard rounded the stone, he could see Knobby's flailing feet as his friend struggled to free himself from the arms of one of those savage clowns.

"H-h-h-ha! What's green, bumpy and dead all over? YOU! He-he-heee, ho-ho!" it maniacally sang out with triumphal glee.

"Can't...breath..." wheezed Knobby. He gasped and thrashed about to get free, but the clown squeezed tighter and laughed louder.

Though too frightened to move, Bernard wasn't too frightened to think. Besides horrible thoughts caked in fear, the notion came to him that with the clown facing the other way he might escape unnoticed. He might escape, that is, if he were a friend-abandoning scoundrel. He wasn't, but neither was he strong or brave. What could he do? While his mind raced for an answer another part of it subconsciously contemplated the clown's attire. That may sound strange, but not so strange once you understand why. You see, the clown wore a waistcoat several sizes too small, an unfortunate garment choice for him, because it revealed his pants pockets quite plainly, and in that vicinity there was a distinct bulge with a wet spot that emanated from it running down the leg. That confirmed it for Bernard, who greedily consumed the local newspaper on a daily basis and had once read a scathing review, by the paper's child editor and publisher, of a birthday party that included a tell-all exposé on a clown act. The article went into great detail on the "nefarious practices of a heinous huckster known as Twinkles," revealing in minute detail the dark secrets of the clown industry. Armed with this knowledge, Bernard summoned the courage to leap forwards upon the clown's back thrusting his hand into its pocket and grabbing hold of the ball he knew would be there. With his other hand he reached over the clowns shoulder and grasped the purple carnation in the waistcoat lapel. He turned the flower on the clown and gave the ball a squeeze that sent a gush of water blasting into its face. The clown, shrieking like a tortured animal, dropped Knobby and went tumbling backwards. The wretched thing screeched and clawed at its own face, now make-up-less and naked for all to see. Bernard scrambled out from underneath the writhing clown with Knobby's help and as they sped away he turned and caught a glimpse of the thing partially de-make-upped, a sight too awful to relate.

The two friends moved more cautiously now, ducking and dashing from stone to stone. A flash of polka dots just ahead sent them scampering behind a stone, barely avoiding a rainbow afro-wigged marauder. While waiting for Knobby's signal to move again, Bernard spied an auspicious opportunity.

"Here! Look," he whispered, tugging at Knobby's arm. At their feet, not a step away, a large hole opened before them. Without a second's thought, they climbed into it, sliding down a steep incline of pungent, newly dug soil into a roundish tunnel just wide and tall enough for them to crouch in. Bernard and Knobby huddled together there just outside the beam of light streaming down from the opening. The tunnel went deeper back into the dark, cold earth, but some unseen-though-intangibly-present foreboding kept them rooted to the spot, refusing to venture any further. In their underground hideout they stood for a time listening to the reverberations of the thumping clown feet above.

"I've often wondered what it would be like to be a jerboa," said Bernard in wonder, though in a hushed tone respectful of their current situation.

"Is that so," said a distracted Knobby out of politeness as his eyes scanned the opening. Then not wanting to be rude, he asked, "What ever is a jerboa?"

"It's a sort of kangaroo mouse like rodent with enormous feet for hopping and often a large set of ears. Boy, what they must hear! Them clowns pounding about would stir up such a maddening ruckus for those poor little beggars in their dirty underground burrows."

"Yes, it does sound like an awful lot of them, doesn't it?" agreed Knobby, again mostly out of politeness. His attention was almost entirely upon the opening, while Bernard's wandered enough to consider their immediate surroundings. There wasn't much to see other than a few roots and the occasional exposed rock hanging from the tunnel ceiling and walls. All around their feet were scattered brown-gray, tuber-like objects that appeared hard as rock to Bernard's prying toe.

"Bernard?" asked Knobby in a long, drawn out manner that indicated to Bernard that his friend was in the midst of a great deal of ongoing thought. "You don't suppose one of your jerboa's created this rather large hole we're currently inhabiting?"

"Oh no, I doubt it very much," said Bernard repressing his amusement at the very idea. "They tend to live in arid climes, the African desert and such. Not to mention, they're no larger than a sparrow. One would fit right in the palm of your hand. I doubt very much a jerboa could build such a large place." Bernard stretched out his arms, measuring the width of the tunnel.

"Even so, something built it." The truth of Knobby's statement hit Bernard with its chilling reality. They both looked back into the dark of the tunnel beyond. It dawned on them that they were uninvited guests who'd barged into the home of something with strong claws, probably two pairs of them as well as a good set of teeth to boot. They agreed that their current position could only be quite a temporary arrangement. Yet, if they couldn't stay, going back up didn't seem like a much better alternative. The footsteps crisscrossed above them and the horns hadn't stopped honking. The two friends put their heads together figuratively to think of a way out of their predicament. While Knobby thought of the best direction in which to make a run for it, Bernard tried to remember something useful from the newspaper article he'd read, his only real source of information on clown-related matters.

"A birthday party!" he blurted out, smacking his hands together just a little too loud. Knobby put a finger to his lips, Bernard froze and both went silent. They looked to the opening above and listened towards the darkness of the tunnel. The only thing they heard were the thumps of the feet and the horns. It had been a loud hand smack and they were lucky to remain undetected.

"A party?" murmured Knobby incredulously, giving his friend a doubtful look, afraid that perhaps Bernard's nerves had given out and he'd gone batty. But Bernard soon allayed his fears by relating from the article that clowns are innately attracted to children's birthday parties.

"If we could get them to think there was a children's party somewhere away from here, it might give us the chance to slip away!" Knobby thought it was an excellent idea, but neither of them could think of how to go about getting it done.

"Perhaps a sign?" Bernard eventually suggested, tapering off the final word as a pair of flapping feet approached and stopped by the edge of the hole. The two friends inched back into the darkness. A perpetually surprised white face with a bulbous red-nose poked down into the hole and squinted into the dark of the tunnel. Its crumpled pork pie hat nearly fell off and its wide paisley tie fluttered down into its face. The clown sputtered and grumbled uproariously, making a great deal of pomp over the inopportune attire. In doing so, a slide whistle in its jacket pocket slid out and would have fallen into the hole if the clown hadn't caught it in time, playing an ascending note on the instrument as it simultaneously disappeared back up out of the hole. Its big shoes flapped away.

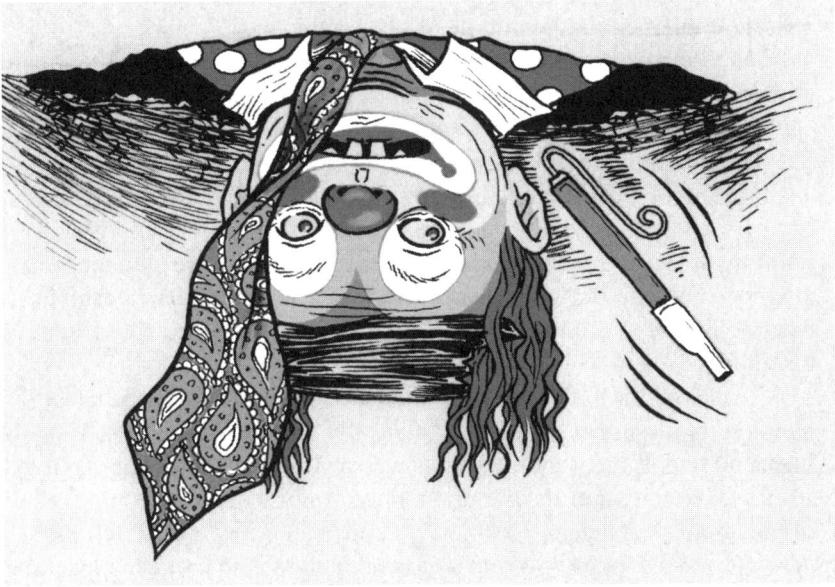

No matter how you look at it...
Clowns have horrendous taste in ties. Fact.

"A sign, you say?" went on Knobby airing out his armpits when it was safe to break silence again. Before Bernard spoke, he felt about his neck, for he was sure he'd partially regurgitated his heart.

"Yes, a sign that indicated a party. And it could have an arrow pointing to where the party is, which should be in the opposite direction we wish to go," Bernard explained. Knobby suddenly got very excited. He thought the idea a brilliant one, as you will read next.

"Brilliant!...Ah, but how to make a sign without a sign or anything to make a sign with?" It was a difficult question. They needed sign making materials and thought on it a moment. Barely a gnat's wing width worth of problem solving did they get done when Knobby tore off his napkin trousers with one triumphant yank.

"With these!" he almost shouted. The long, white pants indeed would make a wonderful sign, a lengthy banner even, if only they had something to write with. They tried a filthy root, a dirt clod, and even a rock all with unsuccessful results. With no other options, they gave one of those odd, tuber-like objects scattered at their feet a try. Once the dusty, dry outer surface had been scraped away, it worked rather well.

17

"What do you suppose this is?" asked Knobby holding up his writing implement in the middle of his graphic design work.

"Petrified excrement I believe," Bernard answered without batting an eyelash. Knobby batted enough for the both of them.

"I'm writing with old poo?"

"I believe so. Please hurry!"

Knobby had trouble moving past this point, but with Bernard's urging the sign was finally finished. It read: "Kidz Partay Dis Wey" with a pointing arrow at the end. Perhaps the misspellings were an intentional attempt to be hip. Bernard wasn't sure, because he also had reason to believe his friend might be semi-illiterate. The two things could so easily be confused.

"Now for the hard part," said Knobby, referring to the task of hanging up the sign somewhere visible, yet without being seen. Wrapping it around one of the standing stones was really their only option, but that would take the two of them to get it done and it would take time. The idea of being out there again, completely exposed to view, made Bernard nervous and, as they edged closer to the opening and crouched listening for clowns, he tooted. Knobby, more the man of action, had them up and out of the hole. They wrapped the trouser legs around the nearest stone so the words written in large letters across each leg was upright and readable, then tied their makeshift sign off at the cuffs with the waistband drawstring. Bernard kept watch while Knobby's fumbling fingers affixed the knot, then they leapt back down into the hole, a jump that had the both of them rubbing the various soar parts of their bodies that had the misfortune of landing first.

In the dark of the tunnel, Knobby rested with his hands on his naked knees and Bernard leaned back clutching his heaving chest. Both were temporarily winded, more from the anxiety of the situation than exertion. They tried their best to keep the noise of their labored breathing to a minimum so as to hear and not be heard. The clowns' footfalls were now few and far off. They might've given up the chase, thought Bernard with a simmer of hope warming his heart.

That hope was iced by trepidation for the uncertainty of their plan when they heard the distinct thump and flap of a set of clown shoes approach and stop near the hole. The two friends huddled as far back into the dark of the tunnel as they dared. Bernard tried to split his hearing in two with one ear for the clown and one for the gigantic jerboa or whatever enormous varmint created the tunnel. Relative silence entered both of his ears for what seemed an interminable amount of time. *HONK!* Bernard and

Knobby jumped at the blare of the clown's horn. *HONK! HONK! HONK!* It went on honking and didn't stop until clumps of dirt and rocks fell from the ceiling under the pounding of stomping clown feet rushing towards them. The trembling earth collapsed about them and would've buried them had the stomping not subsided. The mouth of the tunnel, shaded by clown shadows, cast down into the hole flickering stabs of sunlight until even that was extinguished. The two friends could neither see nor hear much for a tense few seconds. A giddy giggling broke out and spread amongst the clowns. It grew into very silly laughter that flowed like a wave crashing along the beach as the whole gang of them took off with the rumbling magnitude of a buffalo stampede. When the uproar finally died away, Bernard and Knobby let out relieved sighs that were curtailed by a high-pitched screech out of the darkness farther down the tunnel. They scurried up and out of the hole and ran in the opposite direction from which the arrow on their sign pointed.

Not until they were in sight of the windmill again did their pace slow to a walk. Nearly exhausted, Bernard all but insisted they stop and rest under a fosse tree. Knobby was in a suggestible frame of mind for just such a thing, so they plopped down with their backs against the trunk. The tree's shimmering leaves and gyrating limbs captured their attention and instantly held them entranced in a dangerous, near-catatonic state. Anyone could have walked right up, tweaked their noses and they wouldn't have realized what was going on until it was too late. The fosse tree itself was harmless, but harm could come to those held captive to its delights. Such was the case with Rudolph Smudginsky. All the earthly remains left of Mr. Smudginsky were some of his bones piled on the opposite side of the tree. Years ago he'd traveled all the way to grand ole Gary, Indiana to see a show there called "Chicago." So enraptured by the play and the entertainment world in general was he that when he got back to Spritzerville he was dissatisfied by the almost entertainment-less town. Unfortunately, one day he came upon the fosse tree and was so entranced by its mesmerizing sway and shimmering jazz-hand leaves that he sat down under it with a big daydreamy smile and refused to leave that spot until the day he died.

Being a man who demanded less excitement in his life than most, Bernard had had his fill of the fosse tree. However, Knobby wore that dazed Smudginsky smile.

"Come along," commanded Bernard, tugging Knobby by the wrists until he got to his feet and shuffled off.

"I'm a dead man, Beanie," said Knobby when the tree was out of sight and he'd come to his senses. "O'Weeny will have me one way or another."

"Nonsense," replied Bernard. "Once the Kaiser's calmed a bit, you can have another go at it." Knobby stared at him as if he was crazy.

"I might be two brains short of a double brain bonanza cake, but I have more brains than that!"

"I wasn't suggesting we go back. But you could send him a message via the P.O.," said Bernard, referring to the Parrot Office, the government's delivery service wing.

"Put it straight out of your mind." Knobby gave him a look of finality that ended all discussion on the matter. Bernard did put it out of his mind, unfortunately the next thing that popped into it was that he was absolutely starving. He could've devoured any sort of meat or dairy product right about then, and being a man who would unintentionally speak his mind on such matters, he said, "I sure could go for a lovely sausage or bit of cheese right about now."

"Will this do?" asked Knobby, producing from his greasy shirt pocket two rashers of delicious bacon. "One should never be without, is my bacon motto!" As the two friends sat on the first available rock and ate their savory snack their spirits revived to something at least approaching their naturally pleasant nature. Knobby's demeanor rose above absolute doom and gloom, yet even so he still saw very little light at the end of the tunnel. Note: This tunnel is metaphoric, not of gigantic jerboa make.

"I don't know how, but I'll have to find a way to pay the Kaiser back or it'll be the end of me. At best, I can hope to spend the rest of my days in a windowless dungeon, living in filth and dining on flies. And at worst…I'm clown meat."

Knobby was always strapped for cash, Bernard knew. Even if he wasn't thrown in prison, his fledgling catering business, Knobby's Knibbles, would likely collapse because of this and he'd have to go to work at the Owl Factory or worse the Smeltorium, an odoriferous factory on the rough outskirts of town where the poor unfortunates of the village were often forced into malodorous labor. Bernard occasionally worried that he might end up there if his haberdashery didn't improve soon. It provided a constant source of motivation, putting the fear in failure.

Bernard searched the horizon behind them in the direction of Castle Mucusplug. He was afraid they'd been followed, could even swear he still heard flapping feet and honking horns, and would not feel completely at ease until he was safely home again. While scanning about the landscape hoping to never see another clown, he reflected on the day's events. The weight of responsibility settled heavily on his shoulders as he realized that by forcing Knobby to own up to what he'd done to the windmill, he'd assisted in putting his friend in deep financial debt to the Kaiser, as well as putting both of their lives in peril. There was only one honorable thing left to do.

"Here you are, Knobby," he said, adopting an off-handed attitude as he took the coins he'd earned from his feather sale of the past week and placed the money into his friend's palm. "Take it. I can get you the rest tomorrow."

"Oh no, Beanie, this is taking kindness too far," said Knobby, who tried to give it back, but Bernard waved him off. "Won't you need it?"

"No, no. The haberdashery is doing well enough. I can afford it." It was a white lie and he hoped he might be forgiven it by whomever was doing the grand tallying up of such things.

"You're a better friend than a chump like me deserves," said Knobby resting a hand on his friend's shoulder and smiling awkwardly as he fought back a tear. This was a good time to part ways, they both decided.

The sky clouded over and cast the land in gray just before the Spritzerville rooftops were pelted with rain. Bernard tottered along through the village at a power-walking pace on his last ounce of energy.

"I'm home!" he announced as he entered his cramped cottage and stripped off his wet things. This rain on his leaky roof would do his peeling, plaid wallpaper no good, he thought to himself before calling out, "Hello?" There was no answer. He had no wife and lived with no one but his pet. Of the many hats he'd collected and bought for himself that covered every available surface, the homburg resting on the lone cushioned chair lifted, revealing his pet toady nestled under it. The poor thing was having one of its headaches and could only manage a half-hearted simper before dropping the hat again. Knowing what it preferred when it was suffering one of these frequent attacks, Bernard pulled the shades and left the living room, causing a loud clatter as he tripped on the hole in the worn carpet and fell into the coffee table, upsetting both it and the hats upon it. After picking everything back up, including himself, he tip-toed quietly out to the kitchen.

"Splat...splat...splat," said the drips, heralding the end of their death-defying leaps from the ceiling to the puddle forming on the faded linoleum floor. Bernard put a pot under the leak. The drips started shouting "Tink! Tink! Tink!" so he dropped a tea towel in the pot and soon they were saying "thip...thip...thip," but at least they were being quieter about it.

Bernard was actually glad for the sound, for without it there would be no sound. The rain had already stopped. The neighbors were all indoors. Gaiety was in no mood to talk. Bernard might listen to some music if he had any, but being a purest, he preferred his music live. Even his clock was silently sleeping. Sitting at the kitchen table staring at the sink, he sighed a few times as he'd already done just in order to hear something, but that was already getting old and besides, he didn't want to annoy his pet. Suddenly he sat up and looked around, trying to find the newspaper. Reading it would occupy his mind until it was ready to be put to bed. Then he remembered he'd already eaten the paper first thing in the morning. Though not very nutritious, the Spritzerville Tattler was filling, an important attribute in a newspaper for one on a budget as tight as his.

Bernard was left with nothing but his thoughts, which inevitably turned towards his haberdashery. The sales at the shop had been pitiful of late. Lending Knobby the money he'd promised would set him back indefinitely, but his word was as good as the last gold coin tinkling out of his piggy bank, the ceramic bust of Sir Francis Bacon.

"Friendship is my wealth," he thought to himself, feeling assured that Knobby thought the same. He wondered what his friend was up to at that very moment.

Knobby was sleeping.

Damn Dirty Hippies

Bernard Wimple, the fairly fastidious and ever so upstanding haberdasher of Spritzerville, prided himself on the cleanliness of his shop. From the polished sign above his door with its shiny letters spelling out "Wimples" to the spotless broom closet in the back, everything was as clean as he could clean it and as perfectly placed as he could place it. Not to steal thunder from that fantastic broom closet, but just one further word about that sign before moving on, if we may. Though it needed frequent painting due to rust, Bernard was fond of the sign, a handmade store-opening present forged from tin by his friend, Reginald Dillon Fitzgerald, who had once considered a career in graphic design before being bitten by the culinary bug. It was a nasty bite, all black and pus-filled, pretty disgusting stuff really, but that's another story. Besides the rust, there was another niggling issue with the sign. Reginald's rudimentary talent for craftwork (in Spritzerville it's spelled "kraftwerk," pronounced kahrahft-verk, and yes, it's as bad as it sounds, which is why we'll stick with "craftwork" and you can go ahead and pronounce it how you'd like) far outstretched his atrocious grammar and spelling. In school, Bernard struggled with the very idea of dangling modifiers and was no spelling bee champ himself, so it took him a good deal of head scratching before he discovered what it was about the "Wimples" sign that didn't seem quite right. An apostrophe between the E and the S to indicate possession was missing. Though the error irked him, it was a marvelous sign otherwise and he couldn't really afford to have it replaced or even fixed for that matter, his business having gone south by the time he detected the mistake.

Yes indeed, money was tight. It hadn't always been. The shop did brisk business in the early days. But Spritzerville was tucked away in the middle of nowhere, the sort of nowhere where passersby were infrequent and everyone in town owned a hat or two or three by now. Customers were a rarity these days. This morning, in fact, his only customers had been a group of nuns who left in a foul mood without buying anything soon after he informed them that he didn't sell women's head garments, not of any sort whatsoever. He often received disappointed looks from women because of this, but these nuns seemed exceedingly annoyed. Disappointing potential patrons was his last desire, but there was no getting around the fact that Bernard didn't sell women's hats. He didn't sell women's hats because he didn't know women's hats. He only knew men's hats, so he only sold men's hats. It was simple and it made sense, at least to him.

"Ah well, it can't be helped," he said aloud watching the last angry nun leave.

"Pfft, yeah it can, man," goaded a mocking voice as if from some far off distance.

"What a rude…where in the…," Bernard muttered as he looked around for the source. He knew it wasn't one of the nuns, for a nun would never use the word "man" in that context, but still, it could have come from outside. He stomped over to the bay window to do a bit of lip-pursing and brow-furrowing as he swung a mean scowl back and forth scanning Main Street. Nothing jumped out at him, which is always nice, but on the other hand nothing obviously rude revealed itself and that was baffling. He quickly withdrew, not wanting to linger in the window too long and give the impression of desperation. Indeed he was very desperate for customers, but he didn't want the customers to know that.

A cursory search about the entire shop for intruders or hooligans or intruding hooligans turned up nothing, so he went back behind his counter and did some quality leaning while considering other sources. Gaiety had been left home, but even if his pet toady had been there it would never mock him. As is the case with all toadies, it never had anything but kind compliments for its owner. The taunt might have come from his upstairs tenant Mr. Myles Thyghmaster, but he was a very polite young man. More to the point, he was quite quiet, being dead and all, or undead to be precise. The lonely bachelor did have a tendency to moan sorrowfully to himself, but that was only at midnight and generally no one was around to hear him, or if they did hear they seldom heard twice. Bernard considered that perhaps the culprit might have been a neighborhood child playing a prank. It may have been one of the village schoolteacher Miss Kennari's pupils, though she didn't have many left and those she did have would've been in the classroom at the moment anyhow.

Opening the door, Bernard windmilled his arms about to shoo out a fly the sisters had let in. By the time this was done, the pupils-as-culprits notion had been shooed away too, and yet he couldn't stop thinking of their schoolteacher, her brilliant yellow hair and bird-like figure. With his elbows propped on the counter and his chin cradled in his hands, he was full-on daydreaming about Miss Kennari's bright, azure pupils (the kind she kept in her eyeballs and not the ones she taught) when the front door swung open and the bell jingled.

"Good morning sir," Bernard managed to slur semi-comprehensibly as he emerged from his dreamy stupor and pulled himself together.

"Huh," grunted a customer, snapping off an extra portion of gruff doubt as to the goodness of the morning. This old-ish man with jaundiced, flaky skin wore a massive suit and overcoat. Vast swathes of cloth went into their making to accommodate a man corpulent to the point of neck-less-ness. His sweaty, onion scent flooded into the shop, preceding his waddling figure and filling up the room most disagreeably.

"Mr. Grasso's the name and scallions are my game," Mr. Grasso had said to Bernard upon their first encounter, adding as an afterthought, "although, I don't play games." Bernard would've admired Mr. Grasso's no-nonsense, all-business attitude, but right now it was making him nervous as this attitude was directed squarely at him. Mr. Grasso gave Bernard the ol' stink-eye, a raised eyebrow and sneer that accompanied an accusatory going-over that sought out signs of drunkenness, having sensed them in Bernard's slurred greeting. Finding none, due to Bernard's complete lack of inebriation, the man commenced hat shopping. His doggedly dour expression finally un-soured itself a trifle when he spotted a beaver. Cradling it with care, he held it up to the light admiring its modest sheen.

Bernard relaxed and even warmed to this cold man for his obvious love of a good hat, not to mention Mr. Grasso's hat buying ability due to his rumored wealth. The possibility of a sale looked very promising but for one snag, Bernard knew that the man already owned a top hat just like the one he was admiring. Bernard knew this because Mr. Grasso was currently wearing it. Of course in his opinion, Bernard's beaver was better by far, more supple to the touch with trim, smoothly flared sides. To his knowledge it was as virginal as the day it was made, no head ever having entered it. The customer studied its velvety texture with the tips of his eager fingers and his caressing eyes, and was about to double his top hat collection when his sneer returned and he dropped the hat on to the table like a flaming hot potato just plucked from a fiery forge.

"Harrumph," harrumphed Mr. Grasso, "filthy." He cast a scornful appraisal over the remainder of Bernard's stock as if assuming the rest of his hats were just as besmirched as his beaver and then trundled his bulk out the door.

Watching with forlorn regret the backside of yet another non-purchasing customer, Bernard rang up a "No Sale!" on the register and rushed over to examine the hat. Plain as day, he found a piece of sawdust just on the inside of the left brim. How it got there he couldn't imagine. "None of the other hats around it are sullied thus. Yet here's a speck. Off, damned speck! Off, I say!" A more thorough inspection of the table just beside the hat's usual spot unearthed a sprinkling of minuscule specks of wood. "The place is lousy with sawdust!" The place was not lousy with sawdust. In fact, the spot with the little bits of wood was only slightly less immaculate than the rest of the shop. However, to Bernard the sawdust seemed to be everywhere, even though there was no more than a sprinkle of the stuff camouflaged into the tabletop.

"Who would come in here to disperse sawdust with the wild abandon of a woodchipper, I ask you?" asked Bernard of no one in particular. "I don't recall a woodchuck giving my beaver a go, lately." Just as his previous accusatorial theories were starting to resurface, his seeking eyes caught sight of a small hole, large enough to jam a thumb through, located in the ceiling directly over the sawdust pile. "Thyghmaster! I would not have thought him capable of such knavery," said Bernard, blinking with disbelief at the ceiling. He cleaned up the minor mess, locked the door and hung the "Back In 3 ½ Minutes" sign in the window, so that he could step upstairs and have up to a three-minute-long word with his tenant.

It being the middle of the day Mr. Thyghmaster was asleep as usual. When he finally awoke to Bernard's relentless pounding upon his door, he appeared astonished to hear the accusation put to him that he'd been drilling holes in the floor, holes that went right down into the ceiling of the hat shop.

"I've always allowed a great deal of freedom to tenants…Hold that thought just a moment," said Bernard. Running downstairs he reopened his shop, stuck his head out the door, saw that no customers were about, then re-hung the "Back In 3 ½ Minutes" sign and went back upstairs. "I've always allowed a great deal of freedom to tenants renting this apartment from me in the past, however I do have my limits and the creation of floor-to-ceiling holes is a limit-surpasser."

Mr. Thyghmaster denied the accusation, but seeing that Bernard was clearly in a huff over the matter, he implored him to have a look about the place to put his mind at ease. Bernard did not see the expected hole anywhere, especially not on the floor where there most definitely should have been a hole. He was quite floored about the hole-less flooring. A little thumb-sized void appearing in the planks would've answered all. Was this some sort of black magic or undead devilry surfacing from the young man's ancestral past, he wondered, though graciously not aloud. Finding nothing but a void of a void, Bernard was left devoid of anything but the need to apologize and exit as humbly as he might. Before leaving, he did think to kindly inquire upon the condition of Mr. Thyghmaster's fez, one he'd purchased at the haberdashery. Mr. Thyghmaster graciously thanked him for his thoughtfulness, as only a well-bred, undead fowl can. He even showed sympathy towards Bernard's hole problem, vowing assistance if needed, and then politely showed him to the door.

Bernard felt embarrassed for assuming the worst when his tenant had always been nothing but the best sort one could wish, especially in respect to being a reliable rent payer, that most charming of qualities a landlord can find in a tenant. In an effort to warm the temperature of his otherwise icy end of the social interaction, Bernard ventured to call Mr. Thyghmaster by the familiar "Myles" as he said goodbye. Then while walking back down the stairs to his shop he vowed he would no longer jump to conclusions when it came to his tenant in the future.

The conundrum of the ceiling hole and his rudeness towards his tenant instantly vanished from his thoughts when the strong scent of smoke sucked up his nose upon reentering the shop. The sight of billowy puffs wafting from his cuckoo clock sent him into a panic. He ran this way. He ran that way. Should he grab a bucket of water and try to put the fire out himself? Or should he call the fire department straight away? He wasn't sure. Just then the clock doors popped open and, instead of Cluckin' Chuck the Cuckoo Bird, a scruffy mouse in a faded tank top flew out at the end of the gangplank as it shot through the tiny double-doors. He nearly tumbled off and would've fallen to his death if he hadn't caught his balance with a deft swaying of his hips and fluttering of his arms. Smoke swirled out from behind him and he choked and coughed until he caught his breath again. Then he wiped the soot from his eyes, dusted off his board shorts and whipped back his bleached blond hair, spotting Bernard as he did so.

"Awww dude, I am soooo sorry," said the mouse with a surfer's drawl. "The bonfire got a little outta hand."

People often use the phrase "flipped his lid" to indicate someone who has become enraged to a great extent. You may apply it to Bernard in this instance, because he was pushing the definition to its utmost. When the mouse appeared in the clock doorway, casually conversing and gesticulating about this conflagration apparently burning between the walls and possibly floorboards of the building, Bernard flipped many a lid diving across his shop, toppling top hats and disturbing deerstalkers in his furiously lid-flipping haste to get at that mouse, who Bernard saw as the embodiment of his business's imminent destruction.

That mouse of course had a name. If Bernard were in a friendlier mood introductions would have been made during which he would have discovered the mouse's name to be Cheddar, or at least that's what his friends called him. All Bernard cared about at the moment was Cheddar's proximity, slouching about at the end of the cuckoo bird's gangplank, completely prone for a good plucking. Bernard lunged forward to make a grab at him and if not for the placement of the three-legged hat stand the mouse would be lost, the mouse would be lost. But as always seems to happen when one is angry and in a rush, mishaps abound. Bernard took a tumble over the stand, which knocked the hats all over the floor, so that he, the hats and the stand fumbled, flopped and clattered into a heap just under the clock.

"Whoa dude, no need to get your panties in a bunch," said Cheddar. "It's all good. We got it under control. Fuzzy whizzed all over the fire and put it out." The mouse's eyes disappeared into its sunburnt face, which spread wide as he broke out laughing. "You shoulda seen it, dude seriously had to go!"

"You don't even know, dude," said a long-haired, tubby mouse emerging from the clock door, wearing a tie-dye shirt and shirkenflop sandals.

"Fuzzy! Dude, that was sooo gnarly," hollered Cheddar, slapping Fuzzy on the back. Fuzzy uttered a stuttering chuckle through a plastered-on grin.

Bernard took an optimistic view of at least one aspect of this whole situation. The fire was out. Now he wouldn't have to call the fire department. When in Spritzerville do not call the fire department. Bernard made the disastrous mistake of ringing them up the week prior when he thought he'd smelled smoke. They took their sweet time getting there, a whole hour of sweet time. That's what you get when you rely on an all-volunteer fire department made up of giant sloths. "Hurry! Hurry!," Bernard had shouted as they slowly rolled up in their sluggish jalopy, still leisurely donning their gear. The oldest of them never even finished dressing. "What's all the rush, Rushy McRusherson? Where's the fire?" the chief had eventually replied to Bernard's flailing appendages and frantic exclamations. By then the smoke had dispersed and no fire was to be found, but that didn't stop the firemen from trudging in with their muddy boots, dragging the cumbersome fire hose through his shop, and then goofing around trying on the various hats once they realized there was no

The Spritzerville F.D.: Always on the job!

fun to be had putting out a fire. It took him hours to clean up the mess after they'd gone.

Now that he knew his whole shop was not going to burn to the ground in the foreseeable future, Bernard's focus shifted. He did not want it spread around town that he had a mouse problem. Wimple's was a clean establishment and that left no room for mice, for mice are not clean. Take for example the one named Fuzzy, standing there with his beard encrusted with spray-can cheese, a beer stained shirt and a pair of cut-off jeans smeared with many years of bbq chicken, greasy chips and pizza wipings.

"Touch nothing," Bernard shouted upon catching sight of Fuzzy's orangey, cheese puff-stained fingers.

Bernard would have to resolve this situation on his own. The first order of business was to extract himself from the hat stand. That took a good deal of furious thrashing about, helped along with a few choice oaths and unfortunate ethnic slurs, "filthy rodents" being the worst of them. He ignored their vocal indignation, which freed up his brain so that it might jar loose other matters, and it did.

"What have you done with Charles?!" demanded Bernard in the sort of shrill voice you hear when you remove a sample layer of your sister with a potato peeler.

"Don't blow your jets, Captain Uncool." This latest annoying placation came from a tall, skinny mouse leaning in the cuckoo's doorway stroking a pointy goatee. He was dressed in a black turtleneck, a black beret and circular blue-tinted granny glasses. The mice called him Daddy-o. "We don't know no Charles, ya dig?"

"Yeah, chill man. We don't know any Charleses," said Cheddar lighting up something that looked like a cigarette, puffing upon it, then passing it around.

"I mean Cluckin' Chuck," said Bernard with hands-on-hips exasperation.

"Cluckin' wha?" said Fuzzy, his heavily lidded eyes going glassy all over.

"The square's flappin' his sausages about that hepcat with the crazy pipes," said Daddy-o.

"I have no idea what you just said. I'm talking about the cuckoo bird," said Bernard.

"Oh, Rocket," exclaimed Cheddar. "Dude, why didn't you say so? He's kickin' it with us back at the pad. That dude hooked us up with some loco weed, man!"

"Ooh, that stuff is like, I mean, wow-e-wow, ya dig?" said Daddy-o with a cynical-less smile.

"Yeah. Wow," repeated Fuzzy. He and Cheddar fell into a laughing fit. Daddy-o casually nodded his assent.

"Why," asked Bernard with some hesitation, unsure whether he really wanted to know, "why do you call him Rocket?"

"Cuz he'll take you into outer space, man," answered Cheddar.

"Huh, huh, spaceman," chuckled Fuzzy, sending him and Cheddar into further hysterics.

"That might explain why my clock is wrong so often. It's been getting stuck on 4:20 for some reason," said Bernard. Thinking the mice's laughter was directed at him, he whipped out a finger and shook it. "Well, there's one bird who's going to be looking for a new job tomorrow!"

"That is harsh, man," said Cheddar.

"Ice in squaresville," put in Daddy-o. Both of them looked down on Bernard as if he were beneath them, while Fuzzy stared at the wall cross-eyed. With the Cluckin' Chuck situation situated, Bernard turned his attention back towards the mice and he didn't like what he saw. A repellent idea entered his thoughts.

"Are you," again Bernard hesitated, not sure he wanted to ask and receive an answer. "Are you hippies?"

"Labels. So uncool," said Daddy-o shaking his head.

"Yeah, whatever man, we just like havin' a good time and not be, uh, like, tied down by no one, ya know? Live free or die trying...or um, however that goes. That's our creed...or gredo... or motto? Whatever, man."

"So," started in Bernard, but whatever word was coming next caught in his throat leaving him gasping, coughing and red in the face. He was choking on an idea. It couldn't be helped. Ever since his parents had abandoned him to go off and live the life of gypsies, he'd grown to loath the sort of free-spiritedness associated with the counter culture community. It so often led to egregious irresponsibility. "So, there's a whole rat's nest of hippie mice in my walls, is there?" asked Bernard, his eyebrows rising steadily along with his irritation.

"Watch the 'tude, dude!"

"Scrap the *rats*, fat cat."

"Well," said Bernard with a wave of the hand, "whatever you call yourselves...a colony of mice then."

"We haven't colonized nothin', square. We're a collective."

"You moved into my shop, you're living between my walls, sounds to me like a colony, but whatever it is, you're nothing but a bunch of damn dirty hippies, or worse, gypsies!" retorted Bernard. Cheddar told him to get over himself, Daddy-o called him a fascist and Fuzzy stared at the wall cross-eyed. Bernard held up his hands and closed his eyes. After a deep breath, he said, "I honestly don't care what you want to call yourselves. As far as I'm concerned, by tomorrow, if not sooner, you all will be in the same boat as my ex-cuckoo bird, looking for a new place to stay."

31

What? A caption? Cap-shawn. Huh, huh…huh. That's a funny word.

Afterward Bernard wished he'd said "float" instead of "stay," as it would've gone so much better with "boat." Ah well, we can't all be as slick as Ray Jay Johnson.

This hippie mouse infestation wasn't news to Bernard. It was a dirty little secret that pretty much everyone in Spritzerville knew, but no one would admit. Nearly all the houses and shops at some time or other had suffered a visit from these vagabonds. Regular old mice are bad enough, but there are valid reasons for the stigma the people attach to this particular kind of rodent invasion. For one, hippie mice eat you out of house and home. When they get the munchies, your snacks are toast. Literally, toast is often all you're left to snack upon. Secondly, they're complete slobs, leaving trash strewn about everywhere they go. The only time they clean it up is when they burn it in one of their bonfires. Also, their personal hygiene is appalling. They never bath, change clothes, brush their teeth, use deodorant, clean the dirt from under their nails, etc., etc....the list is endless. But perhaps worst of all is their music. They jam for endless hours, playing the same repetitive, mind-numbingly simple songs. And now all this had finally arrived at Bernard's door. His family history had prejudiced him against all forms of hippie and he didn't like even the very idea of mice, so he was determined to have it out with them and have them out of his shop.

"Not only are you starting fires in my store, but you're burning rubbish, which by the way, aren't you and your folk supposed to be saving mother earth or some such nonsense, not burning it down?" Bernard stopped to let Cheddar answer. The mouse just stared at him. He knew he needed a good retort and was busily formulating an answer with drooping eyelids over glazy eyes and the word "uhhhhhhhhhh..." coming out of his gaping mouth. He was beyond understanding. Bernard gave up waiting for an answer. "And furthermore, it was you mice that put that hole in my ceiling, wasn't it?" Bernard looked up as he pointed and saw a mouse face poking through the hole, tiny beaded braids dropping from her headband-wrapped head. "What the deuce?"

"It's for light and fresh air, old man," squeaked the female mouse from the ceiling hole, stressing the "fresh air" part and digging at him with "old man." Come to think of it, she put a touch of spite in "light" as well.

"Yeah dude, it gets hot," said Cheddar. "You want us to bake up there?" Cheddar and Fuzzy started giggling again. "Bake! Get it?" They clutched their bellies and laughed so hard they fell over one another. Bernard had no idea what they were talking about and that annoyed him even more.

"I'll bake you, you…" he trailed off, whirling from the room hurricane-style, while the mice sat in the eye of the storm peacefully smoking, continuing to emit the occasional chuckle. The hurricane swept back into the room wielding a broom over his head. He swatted at the mice. It should be noted that the last time Bernard took a real solid windup swing at something with something was back in high school during the Seniors vs. Juniors coed softball game. With his team down by one with two outs and a man on third, he took a wild hack at a 3-2 ball high and outside, losing his grip and flinging the bat at the first baseman, or basegirl to be exact. This time around no blood or stitches were involved, but the broom did take out his Stetson display. The missed swipe sucked the mirth right out of the mice.

"Hey, don't squash my buzz, man!" complained Fuzzy.

"Uncool, dude," added Cheddar as the two mice strolled back into the clock. The female mouse shook four of her naked breasts at him before flipping him the bird (no, not Cluckin' Chuck) and disappearing from the ceiling hole.

"Bother!" Bernard shouted a little louder than he meant to, definitely loud enough to be heard upstairs and possibly in the shops to either side of his own. "Very well then," he said composing himself and his Stetsons. "I know how to put an end to all this."

With the help of his mini stepladder, Bernard yanked the clock down and there on the wall behind it was a sizable mouse hole, lingering smoke still trailing out. He had half a mind to stick his hand in there to see if he couldn't grab a few of them, but the other half of his mind thought better of it. He was fully attached to his fingers and rather partial to them not being bitten off. There was little danger of that happening as hippie mice generally tend to be vegetarians, but Bernard didn't know that. He stepped down from the ladder and glared at the wall and ceiling.

"Looks like I've got some gaping holes that need filling," Bernard said, voicing his thoughts aloud. "I need a lot of caulk and I need it bad." New gales of merriment blew forth from the hole. A few mousetraps would be needed too, he considered. This would require a trip to the hardware store, and that was not a good thing.

There were many reasons not to like the Spritzerville hardware store. Firstly, you had to pay just to get in and they called that a "membership fee." Bernard called it highway robbery, but there wasn't another hardware store around for miles, so just about everyone in town was a member. Once you paid, you received a ticket and boarded a miniature train, which took you from the entrance down a winding road

34

increasingly lined with large leafed trees to the actual store itself, located within a sprawling compound surrounded by a high wall topped by electrified wire and netting. The inside seemed wilder than the outside. There were flamboyant flowers of the most vibrant colors imaginable blooming from monstrously huge plants out of some pre-historical past. Vines cascaded down the walls and there was even a tree with a tire swing. It actually seems nice, doesn't it? First impressions, my friend, first impressions. The store had a partial roof, so the sunlight streamed in and so did the rain. Most of the new metal tools were already rusted and all the boxed items sat in soggy, dilapidated cardboard.

The owner was another issue entirely. Nearsighted and cantankerous as all get-out, he often screwed up your order. The only alternative was to get assistance from his grandsons. They were big boys, former linebackers for the high school football team, without the skill and smarts to go on to college, but who still had all the balled-up energy that comes with being an athlete, not to mention all the unbridled rage that comes with taking copious amounts of steroids and not having one's dreams of going pro realized. They'd been separated from their parents at birth and raised by their grandmother until she had to be put down, at which time their incompetent grandfather took over the child rearing. As might be expected, they acted like apes, partly because there was no one to stop them from doing so and partly because they were apes. They weren't so bad when they sat relaxed around the store picking bugs out of each other's fur and eating them. Sure, it was gross and there'd be no one to help you with your hardware needs until they were done, but it was better than when they got angry and threw handfuls of their own feces at you.

When Bernard arrived the store's employees all happened to be sleeping. Since there was no one to help him, he took it upon himself to find what he needed, climbing a vine to grab the mousetraps from atop a shelf and finding the caulk almost entirely buried in a hole, to keep it moist he supposed. At the register counter waiting to pay and still no one to help him, his fingers twiddled above the bell next to the sloppily written "RING 4 SIRVIS" sign.

"Might it be better to just leave the exact change?" He searched his pocket for the exact exchange and exclaimed "Fiddlesticks!" when he did not find it. There was nothing for it. His finger tapped the bell so quickly and softly, he wasn't sure he touched it, yet not since "The Rumble in the Jungle" has a "Ding!" wrought such havoc in a sub-tropic climate. A roaring hullabaloo echoed off the walls and a moment later the two grandsons, who didn't like being woken up, were tearing up the place and, as they say, going apey. It was hard to tell them apart because the furious apes had ripped off their name tags as well as the shirts they were once attached to, but nonetheless, one of them came barreling through the nuts and bolts section heading straight for Bernard.

"Help! Anyone? Help!" hollered Bernard as he dodged about the paint shaker and hid for a moment behind a St. Jimmy James Day weekend sale display. When the ape knocked down the extremely faded and wilting cardboard cutout of Pat Summerall that partially hid him, Bernard shimmied up the nearest vine, then swung for the top of a shelf with the toothy jawed, growling ape grabbing at his shoes. He came up inches short and reached out his toes to their utter limit, but it was a near miss and on the backswing the ape caught him by the ankles. As he was pulled down and dragged by the legs across the store, the other ape grabbed him roughly about the arms.

"This is the end!" Bernard shouted. Certainly it was the end of not being battered about by bullies. Definitely it was the end of not being jostled by jerks. But it was not the end of Bernard Wimple as we know him.

"I just wanted some caulk..." The whole sentence was "I just wanted some caulk and mousetraps," but the last part was cut off by the apes' uproarious laughter. Oh how they laughed and laughed. After calming down some, they threw him into a tiny storage room filled with brooms, mops, buckets and something squishy, then slammed the door and laughed and laughed some more. Eventually the grandfather let him go, but Bernard could still hear the boys hooting their heads off as he took the miniature train back to the parking lot.

"I hate the hardware store," he grumbled to himself.

Back at the haberdashery, Bernard began setting up the mousetraps. If you've ever tried setting up one of these nasty instruments of execution, you'll know that they have a hair-trigger tendency to snap shut at the slightest provocation. It happened to Bernard more than once, his pinky getting the worst of it. After firing off a few curses, he examined his finger and an unexpected thought occurred to him. His finger was about the same size as a mouse's neck. He didn't particularly like the idea of squished mouse neck, or squished anything for that matter.

"I didn't start this bloody business, but I'll finish it." The statement was no consolation. Killing was not his business and this business was not good. However, his desire for a clean, rodent-free shop compelled him to perform it. All the same, he would've preferred not squishing their necks and that compassion turned into the mother of invention. An idea popped up. Obtaining a frayed and dusty burlap sack from storage as well as a marvelous-though-costly, blue-veined wedge of stinky Stilton cheese from It's a'Gouda! just down the street, he planned to lure the mice out with the pungent cheese and snatch any mouse that came within reach, shoving them into the sack and holding them in it until he could dispose of them a good, far distance somewhere away from the village, perhaps in the opposite direction of the owl factory if he were in a charitable mood.

He climbed his ladder, dropped the cheese into the sack and was about to hold the sack opening over the hole in the wall when he heard a "plunk, plunk."

"What the deuce?!" The cheese had fallen through a hole in the bottom of the sack. "Probably chewed through by those damnedable mice! Well, there's nothing for then, it's trapping time!" Bernard half jumped, half tumbled down from the ladder. "Looks like this is mine." He shoved the cheese wedge between his teeth, then propped the sack on his head like a turban so his hands were free to grab up the mousetraps and pinch off pieces of the cheese to smear on each trap. Soon his mouth started watering and the cheese began melting all over his tongue.

"Un uf da perfs uf da yob," he mumbled as he climbed back up the ladder to place a trap directly in the hole in the wall. Shifting the traps about in his hands to get a better grip on the ladder, two of them flipped from his grasp and clattered on the floor. "Stew-ped twabs." Climbing down to pick them up, he spotted another hole, this one in the baseboard. He searched the shop and found the mice had dug two other new holes. A mounting frenzy shifted him into a higher gear. He became a trap-laying machine. He also became a trap dropping machine and a cursing machine. The noise of the traps hitting the floor and Bernard's yapper hitting the air eventually drew the attention of the mice. Some popped their heads out from the holes to see what was up. What they saw horrified them.

"Beastly!" some cried.

"Not cool!" proclaimed others.

"He's like a monster!" bemoaned a mouse with a flower painted on her face.

A growing chant of "Monster! Monster! Monster!" came at him from every corner of his own shop. Without the least sign of emotion to show it bothered him, Bernard pressed on with his trap laying. However, he was not an unfeeling, heartless man and couldn't hold out against such a barrage forever. Eventually his festering outrage had him shaking so violently that the sack slipped down over his head and, glaring through the chewed hole and with a mouth still gummy from cheese, he cried, "I am not a monster!"

"He's worse than a monster," declared a brazen, bushy bearded mouse stamping his feet on top of the cash register. "He's as bad as a cat!" The chant of "CAT! CAT! CAT!" rose up and filled the room. All the mice (except for Daddy-o, who used "cat" in a different context) felt this the most vicious slur imaginable, but to Bernard it didn't quite have the same sting. In fact, since cats are renowned mouse-catchers and he himself was involved in just such an endeavor, he took a malevolent pride in it and going so far as to declare in a booming voice, "Heed me, hippies! I will have your heads, one way or another, for I am the scourge of mice everywhere!" Then he realized what he'd just said and hoped no one aside from the mice had heard him.

All through out the rest of the day the mice kept up a ruckus, hurling insults down upon Bernard, who remained stolidly still behind the counter, acting as if nothing were the matter, and hoping that no customers would walk through the door. With much relief, his wish was granted. At the end of the day he flipped the front door sign to "Closed" and although there hadn't been even a single telltale "snap!" yet, he still checked each trap before leaving.

"Sooner or later they'll get hungry for this delicious cheese." He leaned close to a trap to sniff the Stilton. His tongue reached out of its own accord for an irresistible lick, but he recollected himself, shooting an embarrassed glance about the room as he straightened up. "Ah well, in the morning we'll see results then," he said with assured confidence as he took up his hat and coat, casting a devilish look around his shop before shutting and locking the door. "Oh yes, we shall see what we shall see come tomorrow!"

The night he slept the deep sleep of one who's put in a solid day's work. Being taunted by mice and tossed about by apes really takes it out of you.

Upon arriving at the shop the following day he discovered that he hadn't accomplished anything. All the traps were empty and the cheese left untouched. Not only that, but his hats were messed up. Not ruined, not even slightly soiled, just messed up. In the middle of the night the mice had snuck into the shop and moved all the hats around. The Hombergs hung where the bowlers had been, the bowlers were bunched up where the Stetsons once were, the Stetsons stood where the fedoras were meant to be, and the fedoras were flung all about the place.

38

"They're trying to get my goat," declared Bernard, "but that's not going to happen, because I'm goatless to the core!"

While tidying up the hats he pondered the empty traps. It vexed and perplexed him that they hadn't even eaten the tasty cheese. What he didn't know was that the mice - themselves vexed and perplexed that their chanted insults hadn't stopped his war mongering - had changed tactics and gone on a hunger strike. Unfortunately, they conducted their protest within their holes and without alerting Bernard, so he had no idea the hunger strike was going on. He also couldn't make out the anti-war songs they were singing. To Bernard it just sounded like a bunch of squeaking.

Day after day passed and the traps remained untouched. As the cheese grew fuzzier, Bernard grew more frustrated, but it was worse for the mice. With each passing day they became weaker and weaker from starvation. Eventually they lacked the energy to do anything more than just sit quietly listening to their rumbling stomachs. Finally, the strike broke down late one night when Fuzzy, having wandered off and gotten totally wasted the day before, showed up eating part of a bean burrito. In the most harmonious show of solidarity, without a word spoken, the collective dissolved the strike, located the remainder of the burrito and gorged themselves.

Afterwards, when they were able to think straight again, they decided to change tactics. Thus, a very strongly worded letter addressed to Bernard was suggested. A few of the faint-hearted and flower-bedecked felt that was too "alpha male confrontational," while a faction of mice dressed in ironic fatigues thought it wasn't confrontational enough. A contingent of turtleneck wearing pipe smokers put a motion forward to draft up an official petition for all to sign, which should state their grievances and demand their rights be heard. In the end they settled on a very civilized letter signed by all that firmly but politely stated their position. It was written on the back of a gum wrapper and left on the counter for Bernard to find in the morning, and find it he did.

"What's this?" he said snatching up the slip of paper, very furious at the mice for leaving trash lying about. With his hand poised above the bin, he noticed the writing on the backside. It puzzled him. He'd never seen words on the inside of a gum wrapper before. "They're awfully small," he said, squinting to read the tiny letters, which he could not truly make out, and mistaking the mouse manifesto for fine print from the gum manufacturer, he tossed it away without a second thought.

The mice confused his actions for obstinacy, which enraged some members of the collective. Since the movement thus far had failed to meet its end, some wished to escalate their efforts. A motion was made to have a sit-in. This was immediately poo-pooed by the militant among them as being essentially the same thing as the ineffectual hunger strike, and instead they proposed a march on the shop. However, this was seen as reactionary extremism by the flower faction and the contentious meeting broke up in unresolved argument. The only thing agreed upon at the moment was that everyone should go smoke out.

That night up in the eves, a dangerously dashing mouse named Edam and a young, impressionable girl mouse named Eve, held a rally to garner support for an organized march. Eve would've followed Edam to the ends of the attic, such was her youthfully exuberant love for him. At least she thought it was love. She claimed it was his strident ideals that attracted her, but his good looks and wealth of charm may have had something to do with it. During their sparsely attended rally, the room, filled with post-bean burrito methane build up, exploded in a fireball when someone lit up a joint. Not knowing the source at the time, it was suspected that a bomb had been detonated by an anti-anti-war spy to break up the rally before it really had a chance to get going. Regardless of the cause, the result was that when the time came, it was just Edam and Eve marching about under the tables and around the counter of the haberdashery.

So innocuous was their presence, so accustomed to mice noise by now was Bernard, and so busily had he been consuming the daily paper that he never did notice the "March on the Shop" as it was dubbed. Oh certainly he heard their chants of "Hell no, we won't go!" but he paid them no mind, having endured a bombardment of words coming from the rafters, the floorboards and the walls for days now. He only wished they'd clean up their language. Nothing frightened off customers like potty-mouthed mice.

The few mice aside from Edam and Eve who'd even considered marching but never got around to it, gave lame excuses like they'd "got caught up in a killer drum circle." Eventually these slackers made up some signs and hung about the entrance to their holes waving their banners and flags, while repeatedly shouting the slogans they'd written. Bernard barely looked up, but when he did he spotted a man coming from across the street. "A hatless man heading this way!" He leapt up, grabbed his broom and made a clean sweep of the place, a clean sweep of mice that is. He held the broom, not like a domestic tool, but rather wielded it like a samurai sword, slashing at the mice and stabbing at their holes in an attempt to scatter the varmints and quiet them down for the moment. The ad hoc "Occupy the Holes" protests collapsed beneath the iron fist of the broom. They fled for their lives, all except for a very wasted Fuzzy, who'd fallen asleep with his head resting on someone else's drum. Bernard spotted him and had the broom on the backswing ready to bring it down on the mouse's head when the customer popped through the door. The first thing the man saw was Bernard with the broom over his head. Then the man looked down and saw the mouse. After blurting a couple expletives that sufficed to accurately portray his surprise and disgust, he turned on his heel and hastened back out the door. Bernard bolted after him, but it was useless. The customer was no longer a customer of his.

Slamming the door, Bernard stomped back into his shop ready to strike down with great vengeance and furious anger the rodents who would attempt to destroy his business. A few of the mice peered out of their holes at him.

"Scat my beautiful babies, here comes Dr. Death," said Daddy-o and all the mice disappeared. Bernard was left alone to seethe like he'd never seethed before, but there was nothing he could do about it. He was back at square one, impotent against the mice invaders. His anger extinguished itself in a pool of self-pity at this realization and he spent the rest of the day lamenting his plight. There wasn't enough money to relocate the shop. As things stood, with the few customers he had being driven away, the haberdashery would not last much longer. So, it was a great relief to Bernard when he arrived at work the next day and found what appeared to be a peace offering sitting on the counter, a dessert square on a plate with a glass of something purple beside it.

"Perhaps they've given in. Perhaps they'll leave now," he dared to hope with a nugget of warm optimism growing in his belly as he picked up the large delicious looking brownie from the plate and took a tentative bite. Indeed, it tasted as delicious as it looked and since there didn't seem to be anything wrong with it he gobbled it right up to the last. Too many days had passed since he'd eaten something so good…or honestly, since he'd eaten anything with flavor at all, aside from the stinking cheese drippings. It far surpassed the newspaper in taste. The purple drink, a wild grape wonder in a glass, went down smooth and refreshing too, just what he needed to wash down the brownie.

Exactly when the laughing started he could not say, but once the giggles began he couldn't stop them. Everything was hilarious. The hat racks never seemed so ridiculous. The register jingling when it opened sounded cartoonish and never got old. Even the lack of money inside it seemed humorous in an infinitely droll way. "A cash register…without any cash?" It nearly blew his mind. Many things started to blow his mind and he felt a great need to have a lie down before it blew quite away. From his vantage point the ceiling turned into the deck of a ship floating upside down in the sky. The light fixture morphed into a single, menacing eye that would not stop staring at him. Things got a little weird in a dark way for a moment there and if it wasn't for the mice, coming out to join him once they realized he was incapacitated and helping to guide him through his first trip, Bernard Wimple might very well have lost his mind.

He was so thankful for their help in bringing him back down that he agreed to grant the mice living privileges within the shop under the conditions that they remain hidden from the customers' view during business hours, keep the place clean and above all, stopped burning trash. They agreed. And so that's how Bernard Wimple came to tolerate hippie mice and the hippie mice learned to see Bernard as something less than a complete bastard.

Sick!

Holding his pet toady, Gaiety, in one hand and a wooden mallet in the other, Bernard Wimple carefully crept with sly, soft steps into the outer edges of Landmand's Grove. The rickety mallet head, giving off a consistent but subdued rattle, let out a loud squeak. After an involuntary jerk that brought him down into a hunch, every bit of Bernard froze, but his eyes. They darted about the gnarled and knotted apple trees. Nothing. Nothing but slow growing grass and leaf, and the merest breeze carrying the sweetly smart song of a scarlet birdbrain from where it sat upon a limb some few yards away rhythmically rocking itself back and forth to its own come-hither tune in order to enable an occasional violent thrusting display of its pink and engorged pons. Bernard gripped the mallet head and handle tight, then tiptoed away. A whiff of hot air wheezed out of Gaiety's bottom.

"Be quiet, you," hissed Bernard. He stopped under a short-trunked, bushy tree. "This'll do," he said in a low hush. "Plenty of cover. No one around to see." He placed Gaiety on the ground at his feet and adjusted the mallet head, screwing it with a grunt-capped twist. It wouldn't stay tight for long, he knew. It was old and apt to come loose easily. "No matter. This'll be quick." His face held a firm, resolute determination. "Look away, my friend. Look away." The toady cast up its eyes into Bernard's own. "You're only making this more difficult than it already

A cheek-clenching moment indeed!

is." He glanced about him one last time. There was no one around. "It's now or never." He got into a sturdy, wide-legged stance, lifted the mallet, took aim and swung, accidentally smashing a fallen apple into the ground. "Oh damn!" He readjusted his aim and tried again. This time another apple flew a few feet and came to rest in the thick grass as intact as a rotting apple can. "Not bad, ey?"

The toady lifted a weak smile for a second then let its whole body droop back down.

"Yes, yes, I know I can do better. But this is essentially my first go. You might cut me a little more slack," said Bernard looking around for another prime apple. A groan and a wheeze of air hissed out from below. "Oh I say, really now! Control yourself!"

Bernard continued on practicing his croquet swings while Gaiety continued sitting on the ground occasionally passing gas. Bernard brought his pet along because he thought it had been looking a bit less green about the gills lately. "A spot of fresh air will do you good. The air about the apple orchard is quite invigorating," he'd insisted the day before as he excitedly looked over his entirely too worn mallet, discovered in the back of Grandma Ellie's shed.

Back in school he'd developed a love for croquet. It was one of the few sports he could manage. He hadn't played since then, but his interest had been reignited a little over a year ago, about the time when he read "Knit Witties Club Monthly Meeting – Topic: Crochet" in the newspaper. He'd shown up and immediately realized his error, but being too embarrassed to admit it he stayed and became the village's best granny-squarer in the male, under-80 class. That was certainly an accomplishment to be proud of in a way, even if there was zero competition and no trophies handed out for the winners. But the main issue was that the crochet club did not play croquet.

On the other hand, the Inter-Village Croquet League had competition, trophies, very little crochet and played plenty of croquet. The only issue in this situation was that there were only four players per team and the village team, the Spritzerville Streakers, already had four seemingly well-entrenched players.

As luck would have it though, a year and a half ago team member Mr. Cowasocke, a 65 year old wheat farmer, lost his arms from the elbows down in what became known as "The Thrasher Accident." The Spritzervillians assumed he meant a thresher accident, but he was actually referring to a terrible catastrophe at a concert for the death metal band, Limb Thrasher, in which a roadie had forgotten to remove the chain from one of a dozen newly purchased chainsaws used by the band members to simulate the hacking-off of the joyously raised limbs of the front row audience members during the show's climatic number, "A Farewell to Arms." Mr. Cowasocke was no longer a hardcore Limb Thrasher fan, nor was he able to continue on as a member of the Streakers, and so, try-outs were held and a replacement procured.

The new player, Esser VonNussen had always seemed like an average, upstanding Spritzerville citizen, albeit with an abnormally large jaw. However, he turned out to be a Nutmuncher, one of those beings that, according to the latest science, outwardly fits into society like any other civilized person, except for an irresistible urge for wawanuts. They also pee out of their tear ducts, but that's not germane to...anything.

"And what are wawanuts?" is a perfectly acceptable question. Wawanuts exist in the Spritzerville area because of the Kacang family, immigrant farmers from one of those warm, lush, tropical islands that make a person wonder why they'd ever want to leave. In a time before memory, the Kacangs came to this land and set down roots on the far side of Weezy to farm the nuts from the imported trees they called the wawa. Being about the size of a coconut and the very definition of round, they provide the ideal substitute for a ball. Their only drawback is their tendency to split into two perfect halves. They also taste like chicken. White meat on one half, dark on the other.

After VonNussen made the team, nuts would often go mysteriously missing during matches that were lost in disgrace or even outright conceded. The deprivation reached such levels that the Spritzerville team had no nuts to play with at all, which made the players terribly sad and led to an inquiry that saw VonNussen's eventual dismissal, thus the need for another round of try-outs.

The latest trials were to be held upon the following day. That filled Bernard with jitters that made him swing high and top-side an apple, spraying a good deal of meal into the air and over the grass. He was already chock-full of foreboding as it was, what with the added tension of trespassing upon the orchard. He would rather not be caught sneaking on to someone else's property to knock about their apples, ripe or rotten.

Also, to his mind, it would be just as well if no one ever caught him practicing. Being bad at sports was one thing, but being bad at croquet seemed just pathetic. Plus, Bernard had the impression that people in general preferred not to see all the hard work that goes into becoming a proficient athlete. They like to think of their all-stars as being naturally gifted. If talent seems only obtainable by those gifted with it from birth, then people don't have to feel bad about not putting in all the necessary hard work. A very comforting notion for the lazy.

Bernard wasn't going to be lazy, not this time. He was determined to get up off his butt and give it a go. He took a few more swings and splattered a few more apples.

"You see," he began saying, grimacing with determination as he lined up a shot, "the key is to know just how hard you can hit it before it mushes up or, in the case of the nuts, before it splits in two." He tapped an apple with great care. It dribbled a foot forward and stopped. "Too soft. You see that, I'm being too careful now."

Gaiety's bottom wheezed long and airy.

"Wooof! If you keep that up I'm not bringing you to the parade tomorrow and I know how much you love a parade!"

The annual Vine Parade was actually a parade of pets. Years and years ago, the area's grape growers realized it wasn't very profitable for them to be cutting down lengths of their vines to provide for the archaic celebration and so the practice died out. In its place cropped up an alternative in which the townsfolk decorated their pet leashes to look like vines, and so it became a parade of pets. The vineyards were happy to continue providing the traditional wine, so the name remained the same. Cheese was included as a natural pairing and that was Bernard's favorite part of the festivities to which he and his pet were mere spectators, the parade community board members having ruled toadies too slow to participate.

"It would be a shame to miss it. It'll be such fun!" Not in the mood for a parade, Gaiety looked back at Bernard with an expression of misery. "There will be wine and cheese," said Bernard, taking another whack at an apple. "I know how much you love the cheese. Then again, it looks like you've put on a few pounds lately and your digestive situation is not what it could be just now. Perhaps you should steer clear of the cheese."

The toady remained silent. Bernard stepped up to another apple and tapped it forward a few feet. He retrieved it and tried again a touch harder. It rolled a few feet and bumped against a tree trunk. Gaiety let out the strangest toot ever. It slid out at first like "skooo," then screeched in the middle as in "teeech," and rippled a bunch of R's at the end.

"The schoolteacher? Yes, I suppose Miss Kennari will most likely be there, that is true. Perhaps we might say hello? Though it won't make a good impression if you're fouling up the atmosphere, don't you agree?" The toady glanced up at him with a fleeting, non-committal look that said he wasn't bothered one way or the other on the matter. "You're playing it particularly close to the vest today. Well, I suppose, if it'll make you happy, we'll go to the parade then." He took a full swing and splattered apple chunks all over the place. "But you must promise your bottom will be on its best--"

"Hey there, you rapscallion! What you think yer doin' smashing up my crop?!" shouted Farmer Landmand through the trees a hundred and more yards away. Bernard could see the scorn on his face even from that distance. Landmand was a wide man in every way, from his teeth down to his toes. Legend had it that he'd stopped growing length-wise when he was nine or ten, about the time he began carrying bucket loads of apples on his head, and because he was still a growing boy with the rest of him yet to come and needing a place to go, he started growing wide-wise, it might be said. Wide-set eyes over a wide nose and mouth covered his blockish head. His body was one big barrel out of which jutted meaty arms and legs, a couple apiece. The man had what the neighborhood folks called "Mashin' Hands," a pair of huge, knotty-knuckled fists that could squish a whole apple in one palm as easy as if it were a wizened grape. He was old now and never had moved very fast on his stumpy legs, but his voice still carried as well as ever it did. As he flung it with all its weight across the orchard, Bernard felt all of its severe condemnation. He swooped up Gaicty and took off in the opposite direction, running away just like he did as a kid when he and his old school chum, Knobby, had been on a fieldtrip to the apple orchard to see the cider presses in action. They'd wandered off from the group and been caught by Landmand chucking rotten apples at one another in fun. Being in better shape back then, he was able to chase them down and cuff them about the earholes before herding the two boys like sheep back to the group. It may have been decades past, but Bernard still felt the shame of it and was sure Landmand had not forgotten the episode. This time he got away and as he fled he hoped that the old farmer's eyesight was poor enough these days that he might not be able to identify the bean-shaped haberdasher in the dented bowler hat.

The next morning Bernard awoke, refreshed and fully alert right from the get-go. In preparation for the day he did some calisthenics and immediately pulled his lower back, so he gave up and proceeded with his usual "shit, shower and shave" morning routine.

"Wish me luck!" he shouted while throwing on his coat. "Gaiety?" He found the toady under his dented bowler looking paler and more bloated than the day before. "Oh mercy, you don't look good at all. Or smell good either." He waved his hands about to circulate the air and opened a window. "Are you feeling okay?" He checked the toady over, felt

47

its temperature and gently kneaded its distended belly. Gaiety groaned from deep within. "Did you eat something you shouldn't've, because you've got a serious case of whiffy bottom and it's probably your own darn fault."

The toady didn't have anything to say to that, which provided all the confirmation Bernard needed. He leaned back and looked down his nose with disapproval at his pet.

"You'll just have to work through it. The trials are just about to start and I can't take you with me, not in this state. And we certainly can't go to the parade with all those people packed together and you stinking to high heaven. Pull yourself together while I'm gone and we'll see about the parade. I shouldn't be long. Probably'll get knocked out in the first round and be home in no time."

When Bernard arrived at The Lawn at the Spritzerville Grounds he was surprised to see there was already a large gathering of participants, league officials and spectators, more than he expected. Certainly all the village came out for the matches, but these were just try-outs after all, and yet the bleachers were fairly full and the sidelines spotted with clusters of spectators checking out the new blood, as well as a few degenerate speculators, those reprobates who would gamble upon anything. Away from the crowd, the three current Streakers stood talking together, all dressed in their argyle sweaters, white pants and wicker hats that made up the team uniform.

But aside from the unexpectedly high attendance, the atmosphere wasn't nearly as festive as the actual matches. There were no banners or blow horns, and the chants were never as raucous. During official matches, the fans wore their supportive argyles and donned very silly hats, not the sort Bernard sold.

The rivalry between villages was heated and the matches could be relatively rowdy and intense. More than one lukewarm cup of tea had been flung into someone's face. Floppy hats were torn off highly coiffed heads of hair and tossed away Frisbee style. One time the Wheelford mascot, a proud and magnificently colored mallard named "Mallet" was stolen, plucked and set free during a match to parade about so that both sides could see him in all his nakedness. Another time a herd of goats was intentionally let loose on to the grounds by a farmer who was sore at the whupping his team was receiving. "At least no one's been trampled to death recently," the league officials liked to say. It was a true claim. It hadn't happened since "The Catastrophic Cocker Spaniel Stampede of '74," and that's more than can be said for soccer.

"Bernard Wimple to the court. Bernard Wimple," came the announcement over the PA system. Bernard's heartbeat quickened with each step he took on to the court. He didn't even notice his squeaky mallet head with the blood pounding away in his ears and the mixed cheers and disbelief that followed the calling of his name.

"There he is, the apple smasher!" The accusation flew at him from the lips of none other than Farmer Landmand, standing along the sidelines with a group of his gruff farmer friends in their scruffy work clothes and holey straw or worn-thin felt farmer's hats, wearing abundantly stained pants and boots caked in mud. Each had the skin of a man born and raised under a merciless sun. Being watched by the leering eyes of these rough, surly men was not helping Bernard's nerves.

"Keep an eye on him fellas," Landmand boomed so that all the spectators could hear, "that one'll sneak on to yer land and turn yer whole crop into cider when yer not lookin'!" That added embarrassment to the fermenting anxiety brewing in Bernard's gut.

The icing of this unpleasant cake was layered all the thicker when he spotted his nemesis the wigmonger, a man who'd moved into Spritzerville to sell wigs. Bernard was certain this man, this heinous man - "The Spritzerville Stain" or "Old Blighty" as he liked to call him - had put a dent in sales at the haberdashery. Rationalizing this theory was difficult since Bernard only sold men's hats and very few of the men in town would buy a wig over a hat. But sometimes when people latch on to an odd notion it can be tough to shake. Sitting in the bleachers with his family, the wigmonger threw about a benevolent smile and puffed out his chest as if the world were his oyster and seafood his favorite dish. Bernard thought for a moment that they'd made eye contact, after which the wigmonger leaned in towards his wife and son to utter something. Whatever it was, they all found it quite humorous. Their laughter irked Bernard as he lined up his first shot.

"Bernard!" a single, wavering voice eeped out from somewhere in the crowd. The tiny cheer boosted his morale immensely. He thought he recognized it as the schoolteacher's voice, but he figured Miss Kennari must have been teaching at the moment, so he put the thought from his mind and concentrated on the nut between his legs. He aimed and jerked back his mallet. On the backswing, the head on his mallet flew off, scattering the Streakers and landing in the crowd. Red-faced and all apologies, he climbed amongst the people, enduring their jibes while retrieving the offending projectile, and put the pieces of his mallet back together. He repositioned himself over the nut and took extra care as he prepared to swing. Landmand's friends howled helpful advice like "Don't bust yer balls now!" and "Go easy on Kacang's nuts!" The same or similar lines were heard from the crowd at every game. "Nutcracker!" was a perennial favorite and always shouted when a player split his wawanut.

Finally he swung. The smooth orb swished over the immaculately manicured grass, much farther than Bernard expected. Far too far. He would need to backtrack in a big way just to get back into position for his second shot. In this, the first round of the trials, there were numerous nuts, dyed blue to simulate the balls of opposing players, placed strategically about the court so that the prospective player had to navigate through, playing the situation as he or she felt best suited the circumstances. Where Bernard's nut lie, he would need to shoot it in a straight line between two others and just far enough beyond to get it in the vicinity of a decent shot back through the first wicket. More than likely the angle would be too sharp and he would have to take two shots to get through, but that wasn't so bad considering the spot he'd put himself in after his first lousy shot. This second shot required a dangerously solid hit that might bring it into contact with another ball. He swung the head back and let fly. His nut went scooting across the grass, so off target that it whacked off one blue ball and then the other in quick succession, sending them careening out of play while his own came to rest square before the wicket. "Bravo!" and "Well done!" praised the Streakers above the cheer from the crowd. It was a miraculous shot, a lucky carom that everyone praised as brilliant execution. Bernard wasn't about to correct them. He kept his focus on his game and after that fortunate escape, the rest of the round went by swimmingly.

"I think I did all right...I think," thought Bernard, running each shot through his head as he moved away from Landmand down to the other end of the grounds to wait in hopes of hearing that he'd made it to the second round.

"Mr. Wimple? Mr. Wimple," rang a voice from somewhere amongst the people. Bernard wasn't sure who it belonged to, but was sure he didn't want to speak with anyone at the moment, preferring to be left alone with his hope and anticipation. That was not to be. Weaving through the crowd towards him was Ned Droneby, a big-time croquet enthusiast and a graveyard shift button-pusher at the Smeltorium, that rancid smelling factory downwind and out-of-sight of the village. Ned didn't make much money and lived in a one-room hovel in the poorer part of town, but he took great pride in his patchwork Cuffley cap, which he'd saved up for over time and bought from Bernard. That purchase, painstakingly agonized over by both buyer and seller, cemented the foundation of a friendship based on that transaction and their mutual enjoyment of croquet.

"How are you, Mr. Wimple, sir?" asked Ned.

"Fine. Fine. Thank you. Well, a tad uneasy to be honest. I'm awaiting the results, you see, of the last round." Ned laughed heartily, as if Bernard couldn't have said anything more droll.

"Of course you are, of course you are, but that's why I sought you out. You've moved on!" Bernard's jaw dropped and he blinked repeatedly. "You're on to the next round, Mr. Wimple! I overheard them talking, the team and all, and they said you're through!" He'd no sooner got the words out than Bernard's name was announced over the PA system. Ned let out a joyous laugh. "Go on, they're a'waitin' on you!" As he said it, he grabbed Bernard in an embrace about the shoulders and ushered him through the crowd back to the court, propelling him forward so that Bernard had to paddle his feet furiously to keep up with the insistent pressure at his back. But for all he could tell those feet might have been tap-dancing across clouds, such was his elation. His expression lit up and froze in a toothy grin with saucer-wide eyes and levitating eyebrows.

Then the cloud was pulled out from under him and he fell to Earth, that expression wiped off by a full-on kick to the junk. Awaiting him on the court for a head-to-head second round game, in which the winner automatically moved on to the next round, was the wigmonger.

"Ready to get your hat handed to you…hat man," taunted the smugful wigmonger, leaning on his mallet like he was the Lean King of Leantown. Bernard felt the sting of the comment, but was too stunned to retort.

"Smirks are really annoying," he thought, then concentrated on the task at hand. He would respond to his rival's taunts with his game.

At the start of the round they stayed neck and neck through the first two wickets. After that Bernard stumbled. An ill-judged hit sent his nut rolling to a stop right up against the wigmonger's. To have one man's nut lay against another man's is a most awkward position to find oneself. Unlike other league rules, the local version of croquet did not award bonus shots for hitting another player's ball. The wigmonger stepped up and placed his foot on his own nut. He was going to tap it and bump Bernard's, sending it hurling out of play. A "snap!" rang out as he gave it a good, solid smack that shot Bernard's nut across the grass some thirty feet, but in the process the hit split his own nut in two and left him staring dumbstruck at the pieces.

It was a harrowing finish from then on with Bernard racing to catch up and the wigmonger firing his wobbly half nuts at Bernard's in a valiant but vain attempt to snatch an improbable victory from the jaws of certain defeat. Bernard passed through the gauntlet unscathed, finishing a few strokes ahead of his deft opponent, who'd recovered surprisingly well and made it closer than Bernard would've cared. The win sent him to the next round along with two other finalists. He swelled with pride as the crowd cheered his performance.

"Well, he oughten to be good after knocking my poor apples all over kingdom come!" bellowed Landmand above them all. The comment took the wind out of Bernard's sails and he slipped away to await the next round in seclusion behind the bleachers.

The delay between rounds was longer than usual. While the Streaker players, coach and owner had their heads together conducting a lengthy discussion in hushed voices, dark clouds bustled in from the horizon. Overhead the swollen faces glowered down upon The Lawn and starting spitting on the people right as the meeting finally broke up and the Streakers announced that along with the three winners of round two, they would also choose a forth person to compete in a four-person semi-finals which would determine the two finalists. Their choice for the forth was the wigmonger. The announcement tasted like a shot of lemon juice in Bernard's mouth, a vile bile he swirled about his grinding teeth while burning eye-holes through the wigmonger and cranking his mallet on so tight the wood shrieked for mercy. His ears batted away the crowd's comments as they flew about proclaiming it to be a well-deserved second chance for a promising player. To Bernard it felt flat out unfair. He defeated the wigmonger and now he'd have to do it again.

"And defeat him again I shall!" bellowed Bernard right as a clap of thunder shook the earth and a bolt of lightning smashed the PA system speaker sitting atop a pole. Rain darted down upon them and as the people and players ran for cover, it took no PA announcement to declare a rain delay. Some time later the Streakers' coach found Bernard half soaked under a tree.

"Try-outs are postponed until tomorrow morning."

Bitter disappointment still coursed through him as he gave the slightest nod in his opponent's general direction and turned to go. It certainly didn't help his mood any when Landmand hollered after him, "There goes the apple cider bandit!"

However, as soaked as he was by the time he rounded the corner into his yard he'd plucked his poor frame of mind out of the pity pit it had dug for itself. He'd done well enough to advance and he was going to have to go up against somebody in the next round anyhow, so what did it matter who it was.

"Hello, I'm home," he shouted, slamming the door shut and tossing his bits and bobs on a chair. "You should've seen me out there today, I was marvelous! Geez Louise, it stinks in here," he said, going to the cupboard and then refrigerator for something to eat. "Boy howdy, I've worked up an appetite." He went back to the cupboard and had another look at the unappetizing oatmeal, then gave up on food and walked back into the living room. "Hello? Gaiety?" No answer. He looked all around and could not find the toady. Luckily, a cliché did the trick, for when he looked "high and low" he found his pet, bloated as a balloon, floating right up against the ceiling.

"Oh, that's not good."

Once he'd retrieved his toady, Bernard had a good look at it and it didn't look good. Gaiety was in obvious discomfort from the extreme swelling and could not seem to keep from passing gas every few minutes, but there was nothing to be done. Bernard possessed nothing that would help and the vet's office was closed.

That night the constant flatulence surprisingly did not reduce the ever-expanding toady as much as one would imagine and the swelling increased visibly by the hour. Distress begot distress and Bernard's hyperactive imagination soon invented hitherto unimagined diseases, which he now attributed to Gaiety's condition. He concocted an equally ill-informed pseudo-cure and, for an almost unendurable stretch, the poor creature was wrapped tighter and tighter in a blanket in an effort to squeeze the awful air out of him and keep it out. All that did was create the conditions for an exceedingly dangerous Dutch Oven.

Exhausted from nerves, Bernard nodded off fitfully and awoke a couple hours later. He unraveled the toady from the blanket and was knocked backwards by the horrible stench that wafted out. When his watering eyes cleared, he saw Gaiety's pallid body lying lifeless and so engorged that its normally little legs were barely visible now. Holding his moaning pet on its back, Bernard watched its belly distend beyond belief until the inevitable release once every few minutes reduced it some and brought a moment's insignificant relief.

"It can't go on like this much longer," said Bernard, fearing Gaiety would eventually succumb to exhaustion, if not burst. He cursed himself for going off to play croquet and leaving the poor thing alone like this.

"Just a few more hours and we'll take you to the vet and he'll make you better." He spoke with as much assurance as he could muster, but he wasn't sure at all. On the one hand, Bernard couldn't wait to take his pet to the vet. On the other hand, Bernard did not want to take his pet to the vet. Gaiety needed one, but the vet, Dr. Grunk, was a dick. He was mean, grumpy and his diagnosis was always the worst-case scenario. For any and all ailments he suggested putting the animal down. That he had any patients left at all could only be attributed to the fact that he was the only vet in town.

Regardless of his misgivings, as soon as the sun rose, Bernard had everything ready for a visit to the vet's office. He tucked Gaiety under his arm and headed to the vast outdoors where balloons and balloon-like objects are free to float up and away endlessly higher and higher out of sight. Bernard hurried back inside, tied a string around Gaiety and fastened it to his own wrist, then tucked the toady back under his arm and made off for the vet's.

He arrived well before the office opened and passed the time pacing back and forth in front of the door. When the receptionist showed up ten minutes late to open up she didn't look pleased to see him eagerly waiting for her. She didn't even say "Hello" as she nudged him aside with her bulk and her bulging handbag. She flung the door open, waddled inside and commanded him to sit with the flick of a finger towards the waiting room. Bernard sat in a preposterously posture-promoting chair. Never was the back of a chair stiffer. The receptionist dropped her massive handbag on her desk and let out a loud "harrumph!" as she dropped herself heavily into a much more comfortable chair. Paperwork was shoved out of the way. Pens and paper clips were scattered. Dissatisfied sighs were exhaled. The woman's gruff disposition and perpetual glower was not the best medicine for a man with a load of worry on his mind. Not until she'd gotten herself completely situated with a half of a cup of coffee in her did she finally address him.

"Name?" The word dumped out of her like filthy gravel from a bucket.

"Bern-nard," he managed through throat-drying nerves.

"Patient's problem?"

"Well um, Gaiety here has a, well, a delicate complaint of a… a delicate nature."

"What? Speak up!"

He did, but barely. She stared at him with a look that said she only cared enough about the conversation to be annoyed by it. "Patient's problem?" she repeated with more insistence.

"Uh ah," bumbled Bernard, then seeing the receptionist's eyes narrow, blurted out, "whiffy bottom."

"Indigestion," she muttered as she wrote.

"Can I see the vet now?" asked Bernard.

"The doctor'll see ya when he sees ya," she growled, although the browbeating he received from her would've been answer enough.

Another man, middle-aged and care-worn, entered the office with a toady of his own, smiling ever so briefly at Bernard before sitting down right next him. There were plenty of seats and Bernard would normally have been put off by someone purposefully crowding in next to him, but the presence of a potential ally comforted him. Sitting side by side, shoulder to shoulder, it was as if the two of them had formed a defense against the receptionist. "She won't browbeat us into a couple craven cowards now," Bernard inwardly declared.

"Come 'ere, you. Sign this waver," rasped out the receptionist, a freshly lit cigarette bouncing upon the bottom lip of a mouth that would do a grouper proud. Bernard cowered on up to the counter, where he placed Gaiety and signed his name. When finished he looked into the disapproving face of the receptionist. Her eyes darted up and his followed. Gaiety was floating around the ceiling on the end of the string.

"Ya think you've seen everything," said the receptionist shaking her head. She then forcibly took the newcomer's name and his pet's complaint, muttering as she wrote down "indigestion" after the man had described his pet's prolonged loss of appetite. When she was finished with him, his hovering backside hit the chair again and his twitching hands pulled matches and a cigarette from his pocket.

"No smoking in the waiting room!" shouted the receptionist, slamming shut a sliding glass window between herself and them. Aside from the occasional feet shuffling and half coughs of Bernard and the man, who'd grown a pair of dark circles around his eyes, the waiting room remained still, silent and almost sterile, all but for Gaiety's "Old Faithful" eruptions every few minutes, after the first few of which the man moved to the furthest chair. Such an unnatural deadness filled this vet's office as compared to others, which are usually alive with yapping dogs, hissing cats and the aroma of urine.

It was an excruciatingly long wait before a distant, unseen door slammed somewhere towards the back of the building and sounds could be heard of someone, probably the vet rustling around behind a door marked "Surgery." Bernard looked to the receptionist, but her head and eyes remained down as they had most of the time he'd been waiting. Her only motion was to stir enough to take a puff from her cigarette. One would think she was busy with office paperwork, but having looked over her desk when he signed the waver, Bernard had seen that she was only working on a crossword puzzle.

Worst

Balloon

Ever

"Wimple!" called the receptionist.

"Please don't put Gaiety down, please don't put my poor pet down," Bernard kept whispering to himself as he entered the surgery. With the shades still pulled and the old, dark wood-paneled walls, black desk and ancient equipment looming in the darkness and sucking up the light, it was hard to see inside. That was just as well, for the dried bloodstains of past patients still remained in crevices on the operating table and where it had been flecked upon the floor and the walls. A grumble and a grunt emanated from the gloom, preceding Dr. Grunk, a squat man in bifocals with white tufts of hair shooting out of his face from every direction. He hobbled out from behind his imposing desk, grunting as he came up close to leer at Bernard and then Gaiety. Bernard leaned back to elude the vet's yeasty aroma. With another grunt and a smack upon the operating table, he indicated where he wanted the patient. Bernard gently placed Gaiety upon the table and held it down, stroking its back. The vet frowned and waved him away. Bernard stepped back, but kept one hand on the toady's back.

"Bah," growled the vet, swiping at Bernard's hand and just catching hold of the toady himself before it floated away. As he was about to begin the examination, Dr. Grunk sneezed and wiped his nose on a crusty, gray handkerchief and then proceeded to probe Gaiety's abdomen.

Bernard thought he heard the vet say the words "gastro," "inflammation" and something that ended in "-itis," but he couldn't be sure, not as sure as he was of the next words out of the vet's mouth.

"It's too far gone. This animal could die at any moment. We must put it down."

Bernard stood rooted in time and space for perhaps a few seconds, perhaps many minutes, he had no idea. He was lost and trying to understand how one day everything could be so absolutely perfect and the next day it seemed as if nothing in the world mattered. He questioned Dr. Grunk's diagnosis. The vet clearly didn't appreciate being questioned and reiterated his diagnosis in brusque, clipped phrases, while definitively restating euthanasia to be the only option. Not the humane option. Not the right option. The only option. Bernard didn't want to prolong the suffering. He nodded assent to the vet. A goodbye fell from his lips and he reached out a trembling hand to pat Gaiety one last time.

"If you're going to be emotional, please leave the room," said Dr. Grunk, scrounging about in a medicine cabinet for a needle.

Bernard shut the door, walked across the waiting room and stood at the receptionist's desk. She looked into his unsteady eyes and then went for his bill. As he waited, the fact that he'd never see his beloved toady again dawned full in the face and he could not bare it. He spun around, dashed back into the surgery and plucked Gaiety out of Grunk's grasp, leaving the astounded vet behind with a needle poised in his hand.

As terribly distracted as Bernard was, on his way out of the vet's office the abundantly stern voice of the receptionist brought bring him to an abrupt stop.

"Your bill."

He took it, promised payment within the required thirty days while wondering how, in his cash-strapped state, he was going to fulfill that promise, then turned and headed for the door.

"Come here, honey" said the receptionist without any affection, though in a slightly softer tone than she'd used prior. She slid a scrap of paper across her desk towards him. Bernard picked it up and read it. In scratchy handwriting was another veterinarian's contact information, the chance for a second opinion. The black hole of despair he thought he'd never crawl out of suddenly opened to let in a little light.

"Thank--" began Bernard.

"Next!" shouted the receptionist through Bernard and the man sitting behind him jumped in and then out of his seat.

As soon as he was outside, Bernard reread the scrawled note. It was an address for a Dr. Upwell of Flickings, a town some miles away. Bernard had never been there, but he knew it was no quick trip to the corner grocer's.

"This animal could die at any moment," rang repeatedly in his ears as he hustled across town towards the River Charleston to catch the riverboat, a common mode of transportation for the people of Spritzerville. It was the fastest way to Flickings if you didn't own a motorcar.

To get to the river he would have to cross Main Street. Having mastered that whole crossing the street thing some decades earlier, one would imagine he'd have no trouble with it. However, on this day the task would prove to be more of a challenge. The annual Vine Parade was in full swing. Leafy leashes longer than could be believed stretched down the street either way as far as could be seen. The proud pet-owning people of Spritzerville and surrounding villages, none of whom were clients of Dr. Grunk, strutted down the street decked in leafy, viney costumes or papier-mâché cork hats while consuming glasses of wine and wedges of cheese they'd grabbed from the refreshment stands along the route. There was no marching order, no rhyme or reason whatsoever to the procession. Instead of orderly single file lines there were leashes up to a dozen or more deep from one side of the street to another. Many were already tangled with dogs, cats and orangutans fighting one another. The occasional flying stick had to be dodged, because certain miscreants watching from the sidewalk liked to wreak havoc by tempting the dogs to fetch. Some pet owners and their pets marched briskly, while others meandered. Some liked to stop in the middle of the parade to sniff other marchers' butts, while others stopped along the side of the road to chat with the spectators or sniff their butts. In fact, there was a lot of butt sniffing going on and that wasn't the worst of it. Humping was a fairly common occurrence that tended to bring that portion of the parade to a standstill, as well as causing some distress to the humpees (though not all found it disagreeable.)

It's considered rude to pass through a parade and Bernard didn't want to "cheese anyone off," as he put it, the delicious cheese all around him bringing the phrase to mind. So, he moved along the crowded sidewalk towards the end of the parade, at least hoping he was closer to the end than the beginning. But the parade went on and on, and the further back he went the more crowded became the street. Gaiety felt ready to burst under his arms and his head was disappearing into his inflating body. Bernard could stand it no more. Etiquette be damned, he dove into the procession, juking and jiving like a runningback, leaping over a low leash, and dodging a nippy dachshund, who marched next to a woman and her toady, much to Bernard's annoyance. There were complaints and some name-calling, but aside from a few stinging words, he made it through unscathed and was off for the river.

All decked out with a big, red wheel and a much admired diamond and swirl design latticework hanging from the upper deck, the freshly whitewashed riverboat "Broadway Tights" chugged along like a leisurely whale out for a Sunday swim. But this was not a Sunday and in Bernard's mind this was not a time for leisure. In the past he'd always thought the trip along the river a wonderfully swift ride, but now with the need for speed a necessity, the riverboat seemed insufferably slow.

The riverboat captain himself provided the only real distraction. Captain Luey was a tall, lanky, goateed, cigar-shaped man with a love for the aquatic life and a fish's heart beating away in his chest. Literally, it was a dolphin heart transplant. How it happened and how it worked are questions best left to the experts. In general, the Captain was a stoic man possessing a wealth of random and often useless knowledge, as well as a devastating crossover dribble. The thing about him that kept Bernard effectively distracted was the captain's habit of calling out nautical commands like "Batten down the hatches," "Bear away!" or "Hard to starboard, riverboat crew!" because, as it appeared to Bernard, the Captain was the sole riverboat crew member.

Upon arriving at Flickings, Bernard realized he was in trouble. Having never been to the town he had no idea where anything was. The first thing he did was try to obtain directions to the vet's from the first person he found, a high-stepping, high-chin-pointing policeman. As Bernard spoke - very anxious, preoccupied and with a fluttering of hand gestures - he absentmindedly let go of Gaiety. Leaping up, he caught the end of the string and pulled it back down.

"Phew!" he exclaimed, clutching the creature with both hands and squeezing it just a little too tight. The poor thing let out a torrent of gas.

The whole disgustingly gusty scene was too much for the astonished officer, who thought perhaps this stranger was making a mockery of his authority. He shooed Bernard away.

"Keep on moving and don't stop until you've passed the town limits! And make sure you take that…that thing with you!" The policeman didn't chase him, but he looked angry enough to make Bernard scurry off down the street and around the first corner where he stopped out of sight to decide what to do next. He leaned against the wall for a breather and concentrated, but he was far too agitated to think straight. Sweat poured off him soaking his disheveled clothes. He held Gaiety tucked under his arms like a precious bundle as his fidgety eyes darted back and forth. The stress of the situation even corrupted his good grammar.

"We ain't leavin' this two bit town, see!" He looked down at Gaiety's face, spreading and vanishing into its round body. "We're gonna slip this flatfoot and find that vet or my name ain't Bernard Eloise Wimple!"

He realized he couldn't go back on to the street and risk running into the police officer, so the only option was to take a narrow set of stairs at the end of the alley, and so he did. They put him on a flagstone walkway in front of a café. The walkway wound around to a red brick clock tower and some tight-packed cottages, between which another narrow set of stone stairs led to a busier, more promising street. Here a line of shops uniformly painted with black molding and gold leaf trimmed facades lined both sides of a narrow lane. It was the busiest street he'd come across since arriving. People passed to and fro with shopping bags, entering and exiting the many stores.

"This looks like it might be the main street. I don't know," said Bernard. He got directions from a passerby and shook his hand in thanks. That the man was missing his ring finger was somewhat unsettling, but what really troubled Bernard was that apparently the vet's office was on the other side of town.

Gripping on to Gaiety's enormous bulk as gently but firmly as he could with both hands to keep his toady from floating away, he headed off at a careful trot. The directions proved to be as confusing as the winding streets and within a few minutes he was hopelessly lost again. He kept on the course he felt was right and kept his confusion to himself so as not to upset Gaiety in the least. The poor thing was fit to burst.

A difficult climb through a residential neighborhood, steeply built upon such a sharp slope that he could've hopped on the roofs of the houses at either side of him, carried him up and up the hill until he popped out at the top into a very busy street. Pedestrian and motor traffic whipped by him in both directions. Engines, horns, and conversations shoved in and out of his ears. Shops of all sorts and their signs crowded his vision. Fresh baked bread on one side of him and not so fresh fish on the other side did battle in his nose. With his thoughts in a muddle and his senses overwhelmed he couldn't think straight, so he ducked into the first door to ask for any kind of assistance he could find.

"Good morning! How may we help you?" asked a young woman behind a counter right by the door.

"I'm looking for Dr. Upwell's office," said Bernard.

"This is Dr. Upwell's office and I don't think I need to ask what the problem is," she said coming around the counter to look at and caress Gaiety ever so tenderly. "Poor little toady. What's its name?"

"Gaiety."

"Gaiety," she cooed, beaming down at the toady with two affectionate but sad eyes. They were eyes, Bernard realized, with clearly fake eyebrows above them and he assumed she was one of those women who took the job of plucking hairs far too seriously. She was quite the artist actually, for now her eyebrows looked like a couple of two-inch lengths of scrollwork hung upon her lower forehead area.

"Please have a seat," she said, sliding back around the counter. "I'll alert the doctor of your situation and I'm sure she'll be right with you."

Indeed she was right with him. Dr. Upwell came out almost immediately into the waiting room filled with yapping dogs, hissing cats and the faint scent of fresh urine to have a quick look at Gaiety. Then with a smile and a wave she sent Bernard through to her operating room and remained behind a moment to explain the situation and placate the remaining patients, making them understand with a few tactful words the urgent need to advance Bernard and his pet to the front of the queue due to the life-or-death severity of Gaiety's case.

The well-lit, spotless operating room with all its shiny steel equipment was dazzling, but it might as well have been Dr. Grunk's gloomy cavern for all Bernard cared. Nothing else mattered but whether Gaiety survived. He damned himself for his negligence in letting his little toady suffer so and let loose his self-loathing upon his innards.

"I wish you'd brought the patient in sooner," said Dr. Upwell, which made Bernard want to rip out his heart and feed it to the dogs in the waiting room. The doctor worked quickly, prodding with precise hands and

61

nimble fingers, but in the end her diagnosis of Gaiety's condition was the same as Dr. Grunk's.

"Don't say it's too late," begged Bernard. His knee buckled as he edged forward behind clasped hands, sucking up a sniffle and wiping his sleeve across his eyes.

"We'll see what we can do," said the doctor. "We need to remove that sac growing within Gaiety, if we can. It's not an easy operation. There are no guarantees."

"There's a chance?" he asked in a high, wavy voice. There was a chance.

An assistant ushered him back to the waiting room for an agonizing hour of clock watching, nail biting and self-incrimination. Five fretful minutes went by before Bernard could bear it no longer and stepped outside to let the buzz of the street distract him.

He wandered along the sidewalk like a nomad, stopping in front of a shop or sitting for a moment on a bench to watch life pass by with its own cares before getting up and moving on a few more paces. He'd never heard of half the industries and trades that filled up Flickings. Some made good sense. For instance, in another frame of mind he would've very much liked the idea of "home theater," thinking how entertaining it might be to have plays performed in one's own home. The "gas station" was another that seemed praiseworthy for its obvious, practical application. "Had I known it existed," he thought, "perhaps I would've be better off taking Gaiety directly there to the experts." But then there were other businesses that didn't make any sense. The non-profit company particularly perplexed him. "Who goes into business intentionally not to make a profit?" he wondered. "And how," he pondered passing further down the street, "could a company survive if all they did was move. I move, one might even call me a mover, but no one pays me for it." All around him were unfamiliar things. "It's a different world from where you come from, Mr. Bernard Wimple."

The wording of some business and company names confused him by their contradictory nature, such as the body shop that was in a completely different line of work than a place down the street called "The Body Shop." And thinking an exotic scented candle would be the perfect Christmas gift for Gaiety, especially if his unpleasant aromatic issue could not cured, he went into one place that advertised "Brazilian Wax" in the window. An instant later he was pleading his ignorance and entreating them to leave his trousers alone as he backed out of the shop.

62

A shock such as that, upon nerves as strained as his, called for a stiff drink indeed. Hanging over the sidewalk up ahead was a pub sign depicting a rooster and a rack of billiard balls. It was open, so he went in and ordered a hard root beer. Bernard may not have been in the mood for talking, but Gaiety was so far forward in his thoughts that it didn't take much for the bartender to get it out of him. The only other patrons there at the time did what patrons often do in a relatively empty drinking establishment, they inserted themselves into the only conversation going.

"Hate to see a sad soul drinking alone. Will you join us?" invited a very un-broad man sitting at a table a few feet away. Across from him was a man with a dark beard stretching down his long neck. Bernard would've rather been left alone, but he had a motto that went something like this: "When you're a stranger in a strange land it's best to do what the Romans do and not to rile up the natives." He made it up himself. It needed some work.

The conversation flowed pleasantly enough with only a hint of inebriation obscuring its finer points. They asked with great civility his name, origin and inquired further, with great sympathy, the errand that brought him to their "humble little town." Bernard answered their questions and thanked them for their kindness. He did his best to hold up his end of the conversation, asking them about Flickings, but he had trouble concentrating. Not only was he preoccupied by his pet's predicament, but he found himself completely absorbed by the physical make up of his companions. The man who'd invited Bernard to the table sat to his right and was quite certainly a man. All the evidence was there: a deep registered voice, a rather rough face, Adam's finest running up and down his neck, and a way of snorting and swallowing to clear his nasal passages that Bernard had only ever known men to do, with the exception of his Nana James. And yet, this gentleman lacked that signature masculine build in the upper body region. To put it bluntly, he lacked shoulders. The fact first came to Bernard's attention when he noticed the man repeatedly tugging up his shirt, which kept slipping further and further down until finally one of his nipples popped out the top, extraordinary considering the shirt was a turtleneck.

"I see you're looking at my shoulders or rather where my shoulders should be," said the shoulder-less man. Bernard fumbled out a few apologies before the man threw up a halting hand. Yes, he did have hands. They were attached to shoelacey arms emanating without protrusion from the sides of his chest. "It's okay. Apologies are not necessary for a stranger to this town as you are. Simply put, I was born without shoulders. It is a common, almost universal affliction for all Flickings residents."

"I don't mean to disagree with you, but your friend here," said Bernard indicating the bearded man to his left, "he quite clearly is a shouldered man. In fact, I believe he has two of them."

"Yes sir, I do have both my shoulders," said the bearded man, "but the town-wide affliction is not restricted to shoulders." As he said this he turned to one side and lifted his beard to show his profile and a neck that stretched from his lips down into where it disappeared into his shirt with out the usual under-lip protrusion. "I wear the beard to hide it, but you can see plain as day, I've got no chin."

"And I have no bones!" someone declared in a gurgling guttural voice from across the table. Bernard jumped to his feet and saw someone or something occupying the seat across from him. A blob of a man, nothing more than a pile of skin and clothes, lay there like a doughy, deflated beanbag with a flattened head on top.

"Oh good god!" Bernard cried out before he could clap a hand over his mouth. "Ah…oh, look at the time! I have to go!" he shouted as he fled from the Cock & Balls Pub.

Back in the vet's waiting room, Bernard stared unblinking at the opposite wall shedding his bewilderment by slow degrees. Up to this point the day had been all too full for Bernard as far as he was concerned and there was more yet to come. The door to the operating room swung open and the serious looking veterinarian's assistant stuck his head out.

"Mr. Wimple? This way, please."

As Bernard entered his eyes immediately fell upon Gaiety lying on the operating table, as pale as ever he'd seen his pet, though deflated to normal size with flabby folds of skin draped about it.

"The incision will take only about a week to heal, but it will be a month before Gaiety will be 100% and ready for normal activity," said Dr. Upwell.

"Gaiety's all right?" Bernard asked, hardly believing he heard correctly. As if in answer, the toady emitted a couple weak groans that almost sounded like encouragement, its first sycophantic utterance since the sickness began.

"Yes, Gaiety will be all right," said the doctor adding something about dissolvable skin glue to prevent bacterial inflection and a few other details regarding care that she had written down and handed to Bernard, who was too elated to listen. A joy stronger than any he'd known before overwhelmed him beyond all measure.

He was too late for the try-outs, but croquet be damned. Right then he vowed above all else to value his pet, his dear friend, and to cherish the friendship within his heart always, as friends should.

The Grumpling Gobbler

A torment of searing lungs, thumping heart and pained anguish burned within Bernard Wimple's chest as he jogged along the sidewalk as fast as his inflamed innards would allow, a pace no greater than a power walk. Sweat ran over his liver-spotted brow, along his crow's feet and down his drooping jowls. He mopped his face with a handkerchief and cursed his stumpy legs for slowing him down.

Time was of the essence in a situation that could very well mean life or death. Grandma Ellie's message had been quite clear...well, actually it hadn't been very clear at all. "Hurray! Hurray! The expiration date!" the Papuan King had cried. She'd sent the message via the P.O., and a Parrot Post message, though often quick, was not always correct. A single message could be sent via such beautiful parrots for literally peanuts and consequently you got what you paid for. All the same, Bernard was quick enough to realize the bird probably meant to say, "Hurry! Hurry! Before it's too late!" and that indeed sounded quite serious.

The sweat would not stop. His long, twirly moustache sagged with the stuff. Sweating was not on his list of favorite pastimes, but he was willing to succumb to sopping facial follicles in this instance, for although he suffered from a slew of extraneous grandmothers to whom he was neither related nor very fond, this particular "dame of demands" he believed might be the genuine article. Her claims of grandmotherhood were backed up with embarrassing childhood photos, shame-inducing anecdotes and her bizarre-yet-adamant assertion that she'd seen his naked bum on more than one occasion.

Like any grown man, Bernard jammed his past humiliations back into the dark recesses of an increasingly cramped closet of unpleasant skeletons, so that over time a true affection for the old woman blossomed once again. He might not always show it and sometimes not even feel it, but the affection went deep, and so he took quite seriously Grandma Ellie's needs, wishes, complaints, commands and – when she was feeling exceptionally sanctimonious – commandments. On this occasion, he rushed out of the house in such a flutter of nerves, he almost forgot to grab a hat and settled for the nearest thing at hand, his dented bowler. One does as one must, but it is admittedly not a look the town haberdasher should sport in front of such a small, close-knit community. He also felt wholly exposed in his holey, felt jacket.

Ill-attired and agitated, Bernard nonetheless counted his blessings, because the path to his grandmother's lay along the less traveled back lanes behind the Main Street shops of the tiny village of Spritzerville. There would be fewer first-stone casting, upper-crust socialites dispensing their judgments upon him, yet this path was fraught with perils of its own.

"Like a rhinestone cowboy!" sang the wigmonger's son with gusto while whirling a burgundy bouffant wig over his head as he rode a horsey swing for all its worth in the garden behind his father's shop. Bernard tallied it up as one more reason to be glad he hadn't agreed to the business partnership proposed by the wigmonger, a man he saw as nothing more than an upstart, a new kid on the block in the world of Spritzerville business. He frowned as he passed the boy. The boy beamed a ridiculously oversized smile back at him just like his father would have done if he were in the boy's place. Bernard imaged the boy's father riding the horsey swing, singing and wielding the wig. The image brightened his spirits immensely.

Once away from the village center and the prying eyes that might criticize haphazardly chosen attire, he ventured into a different kind of Spritzerville. Unlike the cluster of houses and shops crowding around Main Street, the homes here were set back from the road and hidden from view by stonewalls and shrubbery. Even so, hazards of a rural nature loomed everywhere. One had to watch out for lap dogs, who were liable to dart from under bushes to have a go at your ankles. And then there were those equally malodorous, loitering country lane urchins, who would rocket out from an open gate and use a stick to take the crease out of your trousers round about the knee area, then zip away before you might return the favor.

Bernard approached another of these pastoral obstacles, one of the many tiny bridges that spanned the insignificant streams winding through Spritzerville like dribbly spider webs. The bellflower-clustered banks of these streams surrounded the tiny bridges, offering admirable cover for the angry trolls that made their homes under the stone arches. Under this bridge, so named "Little Girth," lived a putridly pink and hairless trollish specimen of a markedly menacing nature. It was not menacing for causing the usual mischief of a mystical kind replete with riddles, rhymes, devious deeds, or treats to tempt teensy tots, but rather because it was only two inches tall and thus a menacing nuisance when it got under foot. The people didn't call it a one-eyed trouser troll for nothing. Not only was it monocular, but its chief delight in mischief-making was to scramble up the inside of trouser legs and have itself an ankle appetizer. It and others of its kind would race out from under their bridges, and in making for their victims, were liable to be stepped upon, ending the paltry brutes' miserable lives. No Spritzervillian wanted the reputation of being a defenseless troll stomper, well, aside from Margie "The Boot" Hawkins, the much-maligned, self-declared and seldom-challenged county troll stomping champion these past two years running (and currently incarcerated, it should be added). Oddities such as Hawkins being the minority, Bernard was squarely with the majority on this topic and didn't want the reputation of being a defenseless troll stomper.

However, such kindnesses went unnoticed by this particular troll (By the by, his name was Johnson, if you cared. Don't feel bad if you didn't, few do.) who absolutely coveted the perverse pleasure of suckling succulent shin steaks. He waited with admirable patience, watching his victim approach along the lilac-laden lane, down which Bernard ran without time to stop for a fragrant whiff. When the timing was at its most inconvenient, the troll rushed out from under the bridge lashing at Bernard with its prickly tongue, barbed tail and filthy fingernails, all ineffectually small implements of death and destruction, though good for nicking off a sliver of skin. Bernard hopped and side-stepped in a crazy, quick-footed jig that would've made a Riverdance instructor proud. He considered kicking the vicious little bugger into the water in hopes it might accidentally drown, and in his bitter annoyance he would've done so, but for fear of being caught by the Warden of the Weirdlings, the defender of defenseless magical beasties that always seemed to be lurking just around the corner whenever the urge overcame anyone to knock a gnome into next Wednesday or punt a pixie in the pants. So instead, Bernard swerved around Johnson and splashed through the stream, swearing a blue streak and vowing vengeance as he bumbled on to the far bank.

Whether said as compliment or condemnation, it is a fact to say that Spritzerville drapes itself in the terribly quaint. When being fitted out size-wise, "quaint" usually takes a size small. In fact, when passing through town, one rather rough biker gang's head honcho called it "petite," which would make you think it was small all the way around, but such was not the case. Bernard's grandmother lived on the other side of the village and, quaintly petite-ness be damned, it was quite a long while before he was banging on her door. That long while was doubled due to the doubling of Bernard's midsection as well as the town's many traversing paths that nearly doubled back upon themselves as they wound about for no other reason than to show off quaint cottages and scenic views from various vantage points. Nonetheless, arrive he finally did do and...

"Not a moment too soon," chided Grandma Ellie, a woman as round-headed as Bernard though with a good deal more hair, even if it was white. Her midsection had once been as round as Bernard's too, but that was gone. She'd shrunk in height as well, so that now she stood only as tall as him when she uncurled her crumpling back as much as she could. These days her thinning bones were her most defining feature.

"Oh Bernard," she went on in a more tender tone, "you'll forgive a batty old broad, but I've been worried to my wits end over this milk of mine."

Bernard followed her arthritic finger down to his soaked feet, the toes of which were almost touching a bizarrely dressed bottle of milk he'd not noticed sitting there on the front step. As the full explanation rattled forth from Grandma Ellie's dusty old voice thrower, it became clear that the messenger parrot had been at least partly right: the expiration date of the milk was tomorrow. Her insistence on sticking with old school, un-pasteurized cow juice meant its shelf life was reduced almost by half-lives for every hour it sat in the sun, and the sun would be the reason she'd outfitted the bottle in a frilly doll's dress and given it a toy umbrella.

"Be a dear now and bring that in for me."

That was it. That was all she wanted. The big emergency was that she needed a bottle of milk brought into the house. Bernard plopped the bottle in the icebox, ignored the part of his brain that admitted it was indeed heavy, refused her offer of a glass of milk and left in a huff.

He was thoroughly annoyed. No wait, to say he was annoyed only touches upon his true feelings. He'd been worried to death over the urgency of his grandmother's message and as it turned out, it hadn't been worth getting all worked up over. And this was not the first time he'd been asked to drop everything in order to perform some frivolous task by one of his many grandmothers, who he'd long since lost count of. It was becoming a frequent occurrence of late. Perturbation rose high within him for having fallen into the role of the whipping boy.

"Not again!" he declared in a commanding voice with a single and singularly authoritative finger pointing skyward as he marched up the road grumbling something about how there ought to be laws to limit this extraneous grandmother nuisance that afflicted him. "One, maybe two grandmothers per person and no more! Anything beyond that and a fella should be given hazard pay!"

Full disclosure: Afterwards, those flies totally did it right there on the steps.

Maybe you don't suffer from the same affliction. Perhaps you have the bog standard set of two or the less common three or even the rare four. But an often overlooked point is that most people are certain these decrepit dames belong to them. On more than one awkward occasion many years past, Bernard discovered that the old women he'd always called his granny, gran, grammy, nana, yiayia, nonna, mummo, grossmutter, etc were not actually his grandmothers at all. The oh-so possessive true grandchildren of these ancient ladies delivered this news right to his face, spitefully stating that these all-but beyond-the-grave biddies did not belong to him, that they belonged to (enter name of snotty brat delivering malignant message here), *NOT* Bernard. Well, they could keep their musty-smelling things for all he cared. Unfortunately, his parents cared. At their insistence he continued assisting Grandma Whatsherface and Nana So-and-so for years on end until it became second nature. But on occasions like these that resurrected his underlying dread that he'd be under their wrinkled thumbs for the rest of his life, he wondered how many other chumps in this godforsaken world were also saddled with superfluous grandmas that quite likely had no claims upon grandliness.

"Maybe they're grand elsewhere, but not in the Wimple family tree at any rate!"

The rest of the day went by much smoother and Bernard turned in earlier than usual that night, wanting to get enough sleep in anticipation of an exceptionally exciting day on the morrow. A new hat catalogue was expected! It might as well have been Christmas Eve, such was Bernard's hat enthusiasm. For hours he laid awake, staring at the ceiling, peering at the clock. An hour before the sun readied itself for its daily debut, Bernard finally fell asleep and then slept right into the middle of the morning, only eventually waking because of a "TAP! TAP! TAP!...TAP! TAP! TAP!" like a beefy beak pecking at his front door. He slumped out of bed half awake and fully groggy, slipped on his slippers and shuffled through his cottage, making a wrong turn into the kitchen. Another "TAP! TAP! TAP!" spun him around in the direction of the door.

"Who's that tapping at my bloody door?" grumbled Bernard, not coherent enough yet to put two and two together and Sherlock-up the simple solution to this stumper. A more clear-headed Bernard would've guessed what awaited him and if he had guessed he probably wouldn't have opened the door, but he did and wished he hadn't. There on the other side hanging upside down from his doorknocker was a parrot. Sometimes a second, nay, a fraction of a second reveals all you need to know that nothing good will come of that day. Bernard slammed the door and covered his ears, quick thinking for one in a semi-comatose state. Without being able to hear anything, he could truthfully claim he'd never heard the parrot's message and therefore could not be blamed for not acting upon it. Well, he could and most likely would be blamed by whichever grannie sent it, but he couldn't be convicted in a court of law…unless he was sent up to face Judge Kangaroo. Regardless of the verdict, he would feel no guilt for willfully ignoring whatever unpleasant and misguided missive was entailed in the message from whichever unpleasant and misguided grandmother who undoubtedly sent it. Getting off guilt-free was the important point.

"Go away, you flying fleabag!" he shouted, leaning with his back to the door. "And take your poisonous words with you!" The tap-tap-tapping continued. He tried threats, but not even a claw-to-beak plucking dissuaded the incessant bird. Ignoring it, he went into the kitchen, stuffed up his ears with wax and had a cup of tea, doing his utmost to pretend nothing was amiss. It was no use. The amissedness was overwhelming and he finally gave in.

"Come quick! Dessert is running amok! Grandma Ellie," squawked the parrot, one of those dull African Greys. Reckoning this bird was no "Alex," the famous one of its species known for its wit, Bernard wondered just what in Sam Hill this world class feather-brain could possibly mean by "Come quick! Dessert is running amok!" What had the original message actually been?

"Kumquat deserts are on in gay mock?" If that was the message, he didn't see any urgency in attending to it. That was of course not the message. It barely made sense.

"Come kick the circus awning all month?" Why would anyone spend that much time harassing carnies? He knew that was not the message either. In the end there was nothing for it, but to go see what was the matter. And the sooner he went, the sooner he'd be done with whatever nonsense awaited him. So with much dragging of the feet and an abundance of hemming and hawing, Bernard finally got his butt in gear and headed back to Grandma Ellie's house.

"Once a lackey, always a lackey," he lamented. Frustration rose within him and bitterness boiled over so much so that, when he approached the Little Girth bridge, he kicked Johnson. He didn't care if anyone saw. He didn't even feel guilty. Well, perhaps a little guilty. Though it was a negligible nudge with the tip of his toe, it was a nudge into the stream. Over his shoulder he caught sight of the troll plunging into a bush and pulling himself out of the stream sputtering and spewing. Bernard was glad he hadn't drowned, but that was as much of the milk of human kindness as he could spare at the moment.

"Bang! Bang! Bang!" rang out Grandma Ellie's door. Her house appeared to be nothing more than a modest cottage on the outside, but it was deceptively large and labyrinthine within. If busying herself in one of the back rooms jarring jam, potting plants, laundering linen or involved in any of her many extracurricular entertainments, she likely wouldn't hear someone knocking on the door. To remedy this, her crafty nephew, Mortimer, built for her a doorknocker that used those percussion caps made for children's toy six-shooters. They were loaded up bandolier style so that each time the knocker knocked it literally banged, which is no small shock to the nerves of kindly grandsons like Bernard who come to pay visits to their grandmothers on peaceful Sunday afternoons and who aren't pre-warned about this new explosive contraption. While these grandsons are lying on the ground having mild heart attacks as a result of this percussive pop from a deceptively normal looking doorknocker, it is not particularly compassionate for a grandmother to laugh her tookus off at his misfortune.

"Strange," said Bernard when his grandmother didn't answer the door. Yesterday when she summoned him he found her fretting in the doorway as he arrived. The non-event about the milk was bad enough. If this second summons was even more inconsequential, Bernard was ready to nudge Grandma Ellie into the steam, too. "She knew I was coming," he grumbled and then added a few other, not-very-repeatable-in-polite-conversation words in a mumbling tone so low and gruff that by the end it actually sounded like nothing more than "grumble, grumble."

Please understand, this was not Bernard Wimple at his best. It's a shame that when we are so very angry and upset, especially over trivial matters, we often act in irrational ways and, because sourpuss moods feed upon self-centeredness, we are unaware of how absurd and childish we appear. If people could see themselves when they are at their worst, they would make more of an effort to always be at their best. Blame it on the bossa nova if you wish, but it was probably the lack of sleep and worn out patience that had clearly sunk Bernard into the depths of self-pity as evidenced by the way he carelessly tore away the morning glory flowers from the window closest to the front door and rapped with utter impatience on the glass. Nothing.

He strode around the house snapping out his grandmother's name while trying to see into each of the windows, but the yard about the house was more jungle than yard really. Wide leafy plants and eye-blindingly brilliant flowers grew as they pleased. The combination of the quick crawling vines canvassing the lush lawn and climbing up the house, as well as the old willows book-ending each side of his grandmother's squat cottage drooping fuzzy beards down on to the roof where they hung over the eves and curtained the windows, all this abundance of vegetation made it difficult to see much of anything inside the house. At the back door Bernard bent over and shouted through the doggy door. He thought he heard a faint cry in reply. Perhaps it came from somewhere in the neighborhood, he couldn't tell. Dogs were having yappy conversations with one another at inconsiderate levels just over the hedge, making it impossible to hear anything else.

Letting out a nice, long "hmmmm," he left the door and found Grandma Ellie's fantastically thorny rose bush, spied the spare key within its prickly limbs and plucked it out, suffering only minor lacerations. It was your standard - if somewhat old fashioned - skeleton key, however, his grandmother insisted the more politically correct term "undead key" be used to avoid insult until its true species could be determined. Bernard was pretty sure the old lady was going a bit daft, because who's to say they weren't talking about genera? Skeleton could be a genus under which there might be many different kinds of skeleton species. Honestly, he didn't give a flip.

"She can call it a vampire key, for all love, as long as it opens the darn door." He jammed and jiggled its long pointy teeth in the back door's lock.

Once inside, he called out -- Well now, hold on a sec there. You deserve fair warning as to what the inside of Grandma Ellie's cottage looks like before you're shoved in. Have you ever seen the television show "Hoarders"? Gruesome stuff, ey? Well, Grandma Ellie's cluttered cottage was very much like one of those places, at least at first glance. There were considerable collections accumulating in every conceivable corner, not to mention accruing in the corridors. We're talking glass baubles, ceramic doohickeys and wooden whatsits everywhere. Porcelain dolls were piled into porcelain bowls to make room on the shelf for her passing mallard mania. There were painted pine ducks stuck in nooks, between potted plants, holding court above the hearth and a wide one weighing down a leaning Tower of Pisa-sized stack of Rita's Digestion back issues (Yeah, you laugh, but you'll be a slave to your diet someday, too!). However, her saving grace was that she kept a clean house. We're not dealing with a crazy cat lady here. No soiled newspapers lay spread about, nor fugitive fur balls or moldy surprises of suspicious origin. She perpetually dusted and polished the piles and knickknacks. It's just that the piles and knickknacks were everywhere. Okay, so now that you know what Bernard was up against, let's shove you in, too...

Once inside, Bernard called out, "Grandma Ellie!"

"Here," she called, weak and timid, from somewhere deep within the house. Bernard lurched through the laundry room, climbed in and out of the kitchen, dodged about the dining room, leapt across the living room and finally managed to slide his way into the study. There on the top of a toppley bookshelf perched his grandmother, wild-eyed and shaking.

"It's over. She's flipped. Finally gone off the deep end…or about to," thought Bernard, but instead asked, "What in the name of Gordon Jump are you doing up there?"

"Well dear, it's like this…I called you over for a little dessert."

"A little dessert?" Bernard cocked an eyebrow, a corner of his mouth and his head all to one side, so much so it appeared his unbalanced features were about to tip over and fall off his face. Ferocity flickered. Then his very core caught fire with an all-consuming fury. She'd called him over here again the second day in a row for another frivolous reason, on a day when a hat catalogue was due no less. Bernard was absolutely… Positively… UTTERLY! --

"I wanted to do something to thank you for your kindness yesterday," said his grandmother in her most meek and appreciative tone, "so I made you apple dumplings." Now Bernard was absolutely… positively… utterly ashamed for having thought ill of this well-meaning old woman and his awful mood melted away. "Unfortunately there was a hitch. They didn't turn out good," she said with a look that would give an abashed lamb a run for its money in the sheepishness department after it had done something particularly embarrassing.

"No bother Grandma," said Bernard with his best lip-lifting smile, "they can't taste all that bad!"

"Bless you child, no, I mean the dumplings are evil."

"BWARG!!!" growled a nicely browned though lumpy and vaguely cupcake-shaped pastry with googly eyes, a mean scrunched up face and a wide-open, foul-breathed, toothy mouth aimed right at Bernard, who - acting with lightning speed - leapt off his feet and on to his bum. Though neither graceful nor courageous, the flop saved face, literary, as its teeth just missed his face by a fraction when the baked beast flew at him from between a couple of books on the second tier of the bookshelf. The two of them landed on the floor, the flour-based fiend firmly attached to Bernard's jacket lapel, while Bernard - letting out a shriek just one tone lower than an old horror movie scream queen - swatted away with flailing arms at the dumpling until backhanding it clear across the room with a piece of his lapel still clutched between its teeth.

Bernard scrambled to his feet and was halfway up the bookshelf to join his grandmother when he heard her squeak and suck in a sizable amount of air. The teetering bookshelf creaked and cracked as it tottered dangerously to one side. He eased himself off the bookshelf, his wide eyes searching the study for the creature that had disappeared into the stacks of books populating the floor like a waste high forest. A scurrying could be heard and a portion of the forest swayed as the peeved pastry whizzed by between two novely trunks and disappeared again. A paperback fell from atop one of the stacks on to the floor. Then the stack itself collapsed, causing more noise and confusion as it took two, then three others with it. Bernard, thinking he saw the dumpling zip by from the corner of his eye, judged where it might next pop into view and posed the heel of his shoe over a gap between two towering piles of thick hardcovers. A dead thud behind him like the sound of a grandmother dropping from the top shelf of a tall bookcase, sank his heart. Spinning around, he saw one of her voluminous tomes, The Massive Book of Heavy Metal Metaphysics (a heavy book indeed!), lying with apple shrapnel and pieces of pastry splattered all around it. Peering down from the top shelf above was his grandmother surveying the damage.

Here's a recipe you won't find on the back of a Betty Crocker box.

"It was about to topple off anyhow. Now, don't be shy, " she said, gesturing like an insistent host that Bernard should eat the pastry smeared on the floor. She wasn't kidding he realized with mild disgust, but why she'd want him to do such a thing was perplexing considering that in the past she'd always been courteous enough to offer dessert served on a plate. "Eat up!" she hollered at him.

"All right, already!" Still confused, he lifted the book and had a look at the mess underneath. The floors were relatively clean and the dumpling wasn't dirty, just utterly destroyed. Aside from tea, he'd had nothing for breakfast. And one of Grandma Ellie's apple dumplings, ill-tempered or otherwise, was not to be scoffed at. No, it should be scarfed down. So Bernard did as he was told and gobbled down the biggest, most intact pieces. As he did, he could've sworn he saw the gooey, cinnamon applesauce creeping across the floor into one central spot as if trying to gather itself up.

"Swallow it like a good boy," encouraged his grandmother. He'd frozen in mid-gobble. The goo was oozing about in his mouth. "Finish your dessert, young man!" Middle-aged or not, Bernard felt like a scolded child all over again and although he didn't like it, he complied, pouting all the while.

Over a strong pot of tea (with an extra nip of something a hair stronger added to her own cup when Bernard wasn't looking), Grandma Ellie sat down beside Bernard at the kitchen table, which overflowed with a cornucopian collection of ceramic cornucopias. She breathed a settling breath, then began shedding light on the situation.

"As I was saying," she began in a retiring undertone and barely able to make eye contact, "I wanted to make something special for you. So I, and I feel terrible about this now, but when I made the dumplings I used a special ingredient." She dug in her memory for the name. "It's called Jean Eugene's Soylent Mean Elixir. I purchased it from a traveling chef who'd come all the way from France! He was a charming man by the name of, oh what was his name? It was something like Charles Le'Tan." She pronounced the name with her best French accent, which to Bernard made it sound very much like she was saying *char-la-tan*. "I tell you, I couldn't understand a word that man said, but he spoke non-stop and by the time he was done he'd told me all I ever needed to know about this elixir of his that he promised would do wonders for whatever I baked." The smile that built the more she spoke took a sharp downward turn. "But now that I recollect…" She dithered, clearing her throat and taking another sip of tea.

77

Bernard couldn't remember the last time he saw her so embarrassed and it made him more than a little uncomfortable. He held the teacup up to his mouth pretending to drink long and then looked out the vine-covered window as if something outside caught his attention, hoping his usually strong-willed grandmother would hurry up and regain her composure. A little whimper she let slip when recalling something her traveling French chef had said had Bernard ready to scoot out of the room. The words "May I be excused to use the little boy's room, Gran?" were formed in his mouth when she finally went on.

"Oh, and he might have said something about it being good for clearing clogged drains." A hint of a blush rose into the crisscrossing wrinkles of the old woman's pale cheeks. "But he didn't say anything about specific side effects, nothing as drastic as this anyway." She glanced about wearily for a potential dumpling attack.

"Surely there was a warning label?"

"Yes!" She spun around in her chair with surprising dexterity for a woman her age, then groaned and grabbed her lower back as you would expect a woman that age to do after spinning around with surprising dexterity. "Oh my, oh my."

"Is it that flambago you old'uns get?"

"It's *lumbago*," she said, giving him the evil eye and cursing him with a dose of the stuff under her breath. That was more like the Grandma Ellie Bernard knew and it relaxed and cheered him immensely.

"Give me a hand, the bottle's in the cupboard just there," she said, easing herself to her feet. "That what's-his-name, the Tan man, he did advise I read the label, but you know my eyes. I can't read tiny type. Maybe you can make it out."

"I don't see it," said Bernard after a cursory look around. He was not one of those lucky people who possessed the useful skill of seeking household items in cupboards. She nudged him aside and after much clattering about and letting slip a girlishly skittish "EEEP!" she located the elixir amongst the mass of bottles, jars and various other containers doing a bang up job of containing all manner of herbs, spices and unrecognizable food stuffs, not to mention plenty of inedible ones as well.

"Don't spill any on yourself. Goodness knows what might become of you," she said, gingerly placing the bottle in Bernard's hands. He looked over the label and found on the bottom of the backside a paragraph in print so tiny it was nearly illegible even to his own, younger eyes. Holding it in the light and squinting, he read: "Jean Eugene's Soylent Mean Elixir when used in almost all food products - such as meats, vegetables, confectionaries in the form of hard candy and baked goods (especially pastries), and most everything else except for rutabaga – will cause side effects, some of which may include slight discomfort, headaches, blurred vision, dizziness, diarrhea, projectile vomiting, and untimely death, as well as the creation of unwanted magically beings of a malevolent nature. Warning: Any food products made with Jean Eugene's Soylent Mean Elixir MUST BE EATEN as soon as possible. Do not waste time seeking medical attention."

"More tea?" Bernard's old gran sat down in a hurry, snatching his half full cup and lifting the teapot. "Oh, lovely day, isn't it?"

"You knew about this, didn't you?" he asked.

"Oops, tea's getting low! I'll just make another pot."

He sat beside her and laid his hand upon hers to keep her from jumping up from the table.

"Didn't you?"

"Well now yes, I do recall something along those lines. Yes, yes. That was the one thing he did make sure to mention. He leaned close and said very deep and low, *Eberyting go in dee mouf.*" She said it wearing a whimsical little grin and her eyes shut, as if in the midst of reliving the door-to-door sales call all over again and relishing every last bit of it. "Such a handsome, young man."

"A handsome young man who nearly got you killed dead!"

"Nonsense, he wasn't all bad. As I said, he did warn me about this eating business. He was adamant, though very polite, in saying that everything made with it absolutely *had* to be eaten."

"But why?"

"Who knows, who knows." She got up and stood at the stove with her back to him, making a much bigger to-do over boiling water in a kettle than is necessary. "Something he said about it's the only way to finish it off once and for all. *No-ting verks but to eat it'* I think is what he said. Actually, he might have been Dutch or Belgium come to think of it. It's all one and the same to me."

"I still don't understand, what do you mean, nothing works?" asked Bernard, more determined than ever to finally get to the bottom of this.

"Well," she said, turning to face him, "you know that wonderful character from that marvelous tale, the gentleman that breaks into pieces but all the pieces get put back together?"

"Humpty Dumpty?"

"No…the Terminator! I'm sorry, whatever am I thinking? Not the Terminator, I mean T-1000, you know, from the sequel." As you may have guessed, Grandma Ellie knew her movies. Although she lived like a druidic hermit, she had had a nice home entertainment system set up for her by her nephew, Mortimer, and she liked to "watch a good story now and again."

"These little dumplings turned into…I don't know, I suppose you might call them *grumplings* the naughty way they act. Believe you me, if you crush them to bits it only serves to upset them. Then they stick back together like fresh dough and are more ill-tempered than afore!" She shuffled back to the table, placing a new cup in front of Bernard while laying her hand on his shoulder, "If you ask me, I think they're just angry about their lot in life."

"'Ey?"

"Think on it, dear. The poor devils, they were born to be eaten and that's not a very pleasant notion, now is it? You wouldn't like that, would you Lil' Bee?" Once she'd done a thorough job of tussling his wispy hair she sat back down and finished her tea in the more composed manner that came natural to her.

Now Bernard fully understood why he was here. With something like a sturdy skillet, Grandma Ellie could probably handle the grumplings on her own. Sure they had nasty choppers that might take your nose off if you weren't careful, but they were relatively small and manageable if you could find them before they found you. The main problem was that, as much as she dearly loved baking confectionary delectables such as her prize-winning butternut cream cake or any number of puddings, pies, tortes, tarts, assorted soufflés and, of course, dumplings, all of these things she whipped up with a sort of culinary magic were off limits to herself on account of her battle with the 'betes. Bernard still recalled her plumper days. It was how he would prefer to remember her when she was gone. This thinner grandmother with the saggy skin was new to him, new and somewhat distressing to see. New or not, he knew her well, knew her sugar-intolerant condition and knew what needed doing.

"So I must eat all the grumplings," he said with resignation. His grandmother brightened right up.

"If you would dear," she said, already digging about the kitchen and not a moment later kitting him out in a set of makeshift armor and weaponry that included an apron, oven mitts, a spatula and a colander for a helmet, the last of which he complained was "just plain silly." Her overbearingly protective instincts being what they were, she would not relent, but she knew his vanity when it came to headwear, so she conciliated by putting his bowler on top of the colander.

"Okay okay," said Bernard, tiring of all the fuss and feeling quite ridiculous to boot. "So where are they at?"

"I don't know for certain where the rest of them are, but you can begin in there," she said, gesturing to the cupboard she'd just been rooting around in.

"There's one in there?"

"Yes and a very nasty piece of work it is indeed. It tried to take my finger off!"

"Why didn't you say so?!" He rushed to the cupboard, threw open the door and two minutes later was apologizing for the mess he'd made. Herbs, spices and unrecognizable food stuffs, not to mention plenty of inedibles and the containers they'd been in, covered the countertop.

"Don't talk with your mouth full, dear."

"They're really tasty," said Bernard, running his tongue over his teeth and licking his lips.

"I'm glad you like them, because I baked a dozen." She caught the hint of defeat in Bernard's eyes and continued, "But you've eaten two, so that just leaves ten to go. So you're halfway there!" She patted his cheek in that way she'd done since he was a boy.

Rooting out the grumplings was not going to be easy and knowing Grandma Ellie's house as you do now you can probably already guess why. The grumplings had a million and one places to hide. Bernard took a deep breath and got to work. Cabinets and closets were cleared. Sofas and settees were searched. The knickknack shelves and even the shower was scoured. Bernard had hoped to round them all up and get back to open his shop in time or "a.s.a.p." as that pretentious, upstart wigmonger would say, but the grumplings were proving harder to find than he expected.

He did luck out with one of them though, finding it when he'd gone in to use the loo. It lay face-down, gorging itself on the bar of soap in the tub. When he let out a grunt while getting to one knee, the grumpling dashed for the drain, but Bernard brought his spatula down upon it with all the might of ten fly swatters. The partially-flattened pastry lie on its side, moaning and breathing heavily as soapy bubbles slid out of its mouth. That one didn't taste so good, but Bernard didn't let on to his grandmother.

Another he found impaled up the backside upon a prickly pear sitting on the living room windowsill. His heart cried out for the wretched little thing, squirming and growling in anger, and knew it would be better off in his belly. The extraction was tricky and holding it still no easy task

81

as the writhing, pernicious pastry crumbled and squished in his hand while he searched it for wee pricks.

"These oven mitts are actually quite handy," remarked Bernard munching a piece of apple.

"And you scoffed! For shame, young man!" Bernard couldn't deny it, there had been a good deal of scoffing going on.

"Yes, yes. I'm sorry. You were right," he said, still apologizing minutes later, though now mechanically and with half his prostrate body hidden underneath the kitchen sink trying to reach a grumpling stuck in a mousetrap. Canisters toppled over like bowling pins, leaving him a 7-10 split of mostly empty insect repellent to crawl through. It wasn't that he didn't appreciate her providing him with the hand protection, because those grumplings had a vicious bite (He stifled an "Eeeyow!" as the one he was freeing from the trap bit him.) The main issue at hand being that, as nice as Grandma Ellie may be, she had a way of making him feel like he was five years old all over again.

"Old people's prerogative," he supposed, slipping the spatula underneath the grumpling to pry it from its iron-toothed grip on a PVC pipe. He put so much pectoral power into it that when he finally won out the grumpling catapulted straight up and splattered to bits against the underside of the sink. Bernard rolled over and picked off the pieces, letting some of them drop directly into his mouth.

"Oh, you always were such a messy eater," said Grandma Ellie, pointing a trembling flashlight beam of light at him that blinded more than it helped him see. Grandma Ellie had been right there with him the whole time doing what grandmothers do best, urging him to eat. Like a geriatric pill-pusher she pressured him to "Have another," or "One more," and "Just one more." Then "Before it gets cold!" was followed by "Oh you can't be full yet," and a semi-senile "A growing boy like you needs to eat!".

Bernard shimmied back out. It was best he'd eaten that one then with his head in the dark of the sink cabinet, unable to see the fuzzy, years-old moldy cheese from the trap smeared on the grumpling's lips.

"I could tell those dumplings weren't going to come out right," went on Grandma Ellie, now in the midst of an ongoing, ad hoc state-of-the-oven address. "When I took them out I had one look at 'em, ugly as could be, like some babies you see, cute in their way, but some are just ugly and there's no two ways about it, though you always smile, don't you and say 'oh, precious' and all the while you're thinking, 'Jesus, Mary and Joseph, the devil's spawn has come to stalk the earth! But I never imagined in all my days I'd see a normally peace-loving pastry, one of my own baking go from ugly to downright evil! My goodness, have you ever seen such a thing?" Bernard didn't answer for three reasons: one, the question was rhetorical; two, his mouth was full again; and three, he wasn't in the mood. In fact, he felt quite ill, what you might call "sugar sick" from too many sweets. Just as well then that the trail went completely dead for a time. His fullish belly couldn't handle more. It wasn't used to tucking in to such bounties these days.

"Rather exasperating," he thought, ruminating how his potbelly refused to recede no matter how meager his diet had been of late. He had plenty of time to ponder while walking round and round the house until finally plopping down in a chair.

"I give up. They're nowhere to be found, I tell you." He held his mittened hands palms up and sent his most imploring look Grandma Ellie's way. "Call me a cornstalk, because if you have any suggestions I'm all ears."

"Well," said Grandma Ellie drawing out the "well" like someone who owned a set of taffy-grade teeth pulling a wad of the stuff from between their chompers. "They might possibly have escaped…outside… through the, the doggy door." Bernard meant to shout aloud "Ah-ha!" in an oratory of exasperated condemnation, but he opened his mouth and instead out burst a tremendous belch. Not only did his stomach deflate, but under the withering glare of Grandma Ellie, all of his pompous, hot air windbaggery blew right out of him with a poof! - or literally a "BulaaAAARRRGgggaaa…pheeewww!" It's hard to maintain the moral upper hand when your digestion turns Benedict Arnold on you. In the end he held his tongue, bowed his head and made for the backyard.

The strain between them dispersed the second he stepped outside, where even amongst the jungle-like atmosphere of the backyard it was plain as day that Bernard's grumpling hide-n-seek struggles were about to cease. Working as a team with Grandma Ellie as his eager assistant spotter, right off they caught a couple of grumplings in the overgrown garden desecrating a daisy. Bernard meant to "fly into action!" as the saying goes, but as full as he was he could barely even lumber into action. Finishing off the first and having barely sucked down the second with no rest for his bulging belly, Grandma Ellie pointed out another one for him. Up in one of her multitude of birdhouses, a fat and greedy grumpling sat in a nest chomping down Chickadee chicks while their distraught mother squawked and dive-bombed from above to no affect. Before his grandmother could get the words out, Bernard was off to grab the stepladder from behind the potting shed, where he found another grumpling disgracing the next door neighbor's dachshund.

"I can't stand idly by and watch Adelaide get all kinds of addled," thought Bernard. (Note to reader: Bernard hadn't heard that Adelaide had died a few years prior and that this new dachshund was named George.) He whacked this dumpling-of-the-damned off the dog and thrust the pastry down his gullet, while the dachshund scampered away with a hangdog look and its tail between its legs. With no time to lose, Bernard grabbed the ladder, planted its wobbly legs in the thick grass, ascended and was up to his elbow in birdhouse.

"Oh! Be careful!" cried Grandma Ellie from the doorway. Like most grandmothers, her biggest fear for her grandchildren was that they should fall and break their neck. Even the most miniscule of heights might, in the very least, bring about a mangled meniscus.

"Yaaaouch!" yelled Bernard, yanking his hand back and finding the grumpling still attached to the mitt, it's clenched jaws clamped firmly down. He thwacked at it with the spatula, lost his balance and most definitely would've busted his brain had he not dove from the top step of the ladder and tumbled on to the ground.

"I warned y--"

"You better go inside!" insisted an irritated Bernard in a borderline "bark" that took his grandmother aback. She stared at him astonished and hurt, then walked into the house. "It's safer," he said as she closed the door. Regret spanked him like the petulant child he was being right then. No one should ever bark at their grandmother, even if you're a dog and barking is what you do.

He sat for a good long while surveying the backyard and licking the last of the smooshed apple goo from the oven mitt and his fingers. The bitten fingers received extra sucking. The backyard had gone silent and still. As assured as he could be that there were no grumplings left there, he waddled around to the front yard. Nothing differed. Quietude reigned here as it did there, fully confounding Bernard.

"Three remain, but where?" he wondered aloud. "If not in or around the house, where could the three be?" He stepped out to the road and looked around, hoping to heck they hadn't snuck out into the neighborhood. Not only could they wreak untold havoc amongst an unsuspecting public, they'd be darn difficult to track down. And all the while there would be the Warden of the Weirdlings to watch out for. That jumped up constable would probably classify grumplings as "defenseless."

"Ha! Tell that to my fingers or poor Adelaide!" he shouted to the Warden of the Weirdlings, wherever the warden may have been at the moment. Frustration over his perceived failure mounted. "If only I'd come sooner!" He pounded his fist on his grandmother's mailbox.

"You there!" hailed an officious voice, slinging out the word "you" as if jettisoning an unsavory thing from its mouth. "You would not be tampering with the mails, would you?" The accusatory question came from Mr. Christopher Christopher, the village mailman. Even though his job required no official uniform, he always dressed as if he were ready at a moment's notice to captain the Love Boat. Most people thought Mr. Christopher Christopher was a piece of crap.

"Surely they are correct," thought Bernard as he watched the dark brown, banana-shaped man trundle up the road towards him. Being lectured by a local beacon of self-righteous pomposity was not what he needed right now. Pretending he hadn't heard anything, Bernard whistled a melody-free tune and waltzed away a few steps before scooting off around the corner of the house. He stopped and held a hand to his ear, half hoping a grumpling surprise awaited the mailman in his grandmother's mailbox. No such luck.

"Where has my luck gone?" he murmured as he peeked through the neighbors' hedges. Unfortunately for Bernard's needs, the people in this part of Spritzerville lived by what was once only a saying, "High hedges make happy inhabitants!", a saying they now abided by to a monumental degree. He peered through what gaps he could find, but saw no grumplings. At the backside hedge the vines and weeds choked out all the findable gaps, so Bernard resorted to rooting around, digging through the bushes and poking holes through the greenery with sticks until finally he laid down exhausted, nearly slipping into a food-induced coma. While resting on his side like a beached whale, he prodded with waning effort at the undergrowth and eventually opened a face-sized hole. Looking through he found a grumpling staring right back at him! Much larger in circumference than the others, this specimen was somewhat lighter-crusted and disgustingly coated with dirt, twigs, leaves and lord knows what other debris. After the old spatula treatment over the head, Bernard somehow managed to get it down, though it required numerous mouthfuls to finish considering its vastly more mud-like taste than the other grumplings. Plus, this one's inner filling was less appley sweet and more blood flavored with a stringy, meaty texture and a boney crunch. In fact, without going into further details, which believe me you don't want to read, Bernard came very close to finally losing his lunch, as they say. That would be worse than anything that had gone before, because if he threw them up, the grumplings would not be properly digested, and therefore he'd be forced to eat his own sick. Bernard heaved, caught it in his throat and swallowed hard. He rolled over and collapsed on to his back, letting out a long sigh as he rubbed his tender belly.

"No more…no more," he moaned, but through his slimy mouth it sounded like, "no moth…no moth" with a lispy "th."

The late morning in Grandma Ellie's backyard was a peaceful time and place. The rustling of leaves and swish of grass could have been the wind that breezed over his face. However, the grumbling and irritated growls could only mean one thing. "Is there no rest for grumpling gobblers?" he groaned as he turned his head to the side. Through the high grass poking him in the nose and eyes he saw a grumpling-sized shape struggling through the verdant yard. "Perhaps two?" He lifted his head and sure enough there were two of them, one humping the business end of a hoe and the other gouging the eyes out of a garden gnome. Its cries were horrible to hear. Bernard forced himself on to his hands and knees and crawled across the yard, gripping the grass to pull himself forward. "I'm coming!" he shouted to the gnome. He had little love for their kind, but no one deserves such a fate. Once he got closer he realized it was not two, but three grumplings! With a lurch, he launched himself into a most pathetic dive, only managing to get his mitts on one of them.

The other two fled in opposite directions. There was a very real danger they'd escape, and they would have succeeded if not for the dachshund, George, who vaulted through the hedge like a gallant stallion, snapping one up in his jaws and downing it in a single gulp before tearing off back to his own yard.

"Atta girl, Adelaide!" cheered Bernard, but his joy did not last. Once he realized what he had in his hands – another dessert to down - the buoyancy of the moment sank in him like a happy, little buoy who'd suddenly lost interest in its occupation and decided life wasn't worth floating for. What Bernard held in his mitt was no longer dessert, it was a torturous chore. As soon as the pulverized pastry touched his tongue his gag reflex kicked in and he flung it to the ground. The splattered bits pulled themselves together and attempted to slither off. He picked up the semi-smashed grumpling and squeezed it back into bits to incapacitate it again. With eyes closed and breath held, he gathered up his guts with a colossal effort and finally shoved it in. Swallowing it however was another matter. Bernard went through the motions of grinding it up, allowing the bare minimum to touch his tongue. Along the inside of his cheeks and over his teeth he could feel the grumpling pulp creep like a snail towards his lips. The impish pastry born of dark magic was not only propelling itself, it was also receiving subconscious assistance from the will of Bernard's own mouth muscles. A puree of grumpling squished from his puckered lips in a gross display of "playing with your food." He pushed it all back in with a forefinger, held his jaw shut with one hand and clapped the other over his mouth, then methodically went through the motions of chewing.

While grounding up the final chunks, Bernard had a lie down with an elbow propping him up in preparation for a potential puke and to have a look around. He caught the doggy door swinging out of the corner of his eye. Grandma Ellie yelped from within the house. Bernard struggled to his feet like a drunken sumo wrestler and slogged over to the backdoor as fast as he could in his condition, which wasn't very fast at all. The door was locked.

"Unlock the door, Gran!" Bernard tried to holler, but either she couldn't understand his muck-mouthed words or she didn't hear him, or worst of all, she couldn't get to the door. "There's nothing for it!" shouted Bernard as he dove through the doggy door and got stuck midway through. When he opened his eyes and looked up, there was the grumpling, advancing on his grandmother, her back against the washing machine.

"BLAHGGG!" shouted Bernard. Have you ever had one of those moments when you said something and wished you'd had just a second more time to come up with something better? That was Bernard right then. Heck, "BLAHGGG!" isn't even a real word. However, it did the trick and got the grumpling's attention. It turned to face him with the look of one who's constipated and super pissed about it. Unfortunately, Bernard realized too late that, lodged in the doggy door with his arms trapped underneath him as he was, he was in no position to defend himself. He was too fat and exhausted to budge one way or the other. That baked beast was going to savage his face something fierce and Bernard felt certain he'd come out of this situation with at least one less nose than he had going in. With a furious growl, the grumpling charged, its gnashing teeth agape. All Bernard could do was open his mouth wide and cry out "AAAAAAAAHHHH!!!" And then the oddest thing happened. The grumpling fell right in.

That surprised everyone involved, probably most of all the grumpling. Grandma Ellie's look of astonishment melted into one of pride. Bernard was happy to still have a nose and that the whole ordeal was over, but for the chewing and swallowing, which proved almost impossible. Try as he might, he couldn't manage to swallow even just one more time. The way his bulbous stomach felt right now, he was certain he'd never ever be hungry again.

"Immagonnapuuuke," he slurred through the pastry chunks and apple.

"You can do it, dear. Just eat this one last one," implored his grandmother.

"Nuh-uh," he murmured, shaking his head.

"Bernard Eloise Wimple!" shouted Grandma Ellie in her best impersonation of a drill sergeant.

"Icannahdoit…Toofuff…full."

"Don't you tell me you're full!" The old woman started pounding the side of the washing machine like a drum. "Just eat it, eat it, eat it, EAT IT!" Wanting her to stop that irksome chant was what finally put Bernard over the top.

"Milk?" asked Grandma Ellie with a big, kind smile.

"Yef, pweef…" was all Bernard could manage.

An hour or so later, laid out on the couch having done enough digesting that he was finally able to think clearly and reason matters through, Bernard remarked, "By the by, that was a baker's dozen."

"No, I'm quite sure it was just a normal dozen."

"I counted thirteen."

"I assure you it was an even dozen." She dug out the pan she'd used, the twelve-slotter made for baking muffins.

"I've counted again and again in my head and I always come up with thirteen." He went over it with her and she couldn't help but agree with his figures, yet still insisted on her own. They contemplated this conundrum a good long while and eventually Grandma Ellie came to the following conclusion.

"You must've eaten the neighbor's Pomeranian."

"What? No…"

"They let it roll around in the mud and when it bakes on to its fur it looks very much like a grumpling, now that I think about it."

"Awww, sick!"

Facing another day at the haberdashery without a sale would normally have had Bernard morose as a moose in mourning, but not today. Today he felt as jubilant as a cow jumping over the moon. Today was payday at the schoolhouse and that meant another opportunity at pure joy. On paydays Miss Kennari the schoolteacher would stick around late to clean up, plan the next week's lesson and perform other sundry tasks while she waited for Superintendent Nes to make his rounds and deliver her weekly pay. Being a most regular man, he nearly always arrived at five of the clock in the afternoon. Once again in funds, Miss Kennari invariably made for the local toffee shop, arriving there at approximately five to ten minutes after five o'clock, to use the slang. If Bernard planned everything perfectly and his timing was just right, he stood a good chance of intentionally accidentally bumping into her there, and who knows what might come of such an encounter.

"Oh the memories," murmured Bernard daydreaming about their past encounters as he leaned against the counter with an elbow propped upon the register. They'd once shared a heart-lightening laugh upon discovering a mutual fondness for strawberry drop candies. "What are the odds?" wondered Bernard. Another time he'd offered to walk her home. Unfortunately she wasn't going directly home, but rather for a walk along Hawthorne Lane, a charming footpath with romantic vistas. This unexpected change in her routine had thrown Bernard for a loop. Miss Kennari politely waited for him to recover with an expectant and welcoming smile, but he completely missed it. He did not miss the smile because it was hidden under her beak-like nose - which wasn't really as large as claimed by certain mean individuals who were only playing off of her family name since it sounded so similar to canary - but rather he missed her inviting look due to his eyes being rooted to the candy shop's sticky floor as his confused mind attempted in vain to sort out the situation. His mind failed and his only response had been "oh, good day," before exiting the shop in haste. Not until arriving home did he realize the missed opportunity. "I could have advised her on the best views! Darn my muddled brain," he said at the time. Then a few days later he said, "Wait a minute, I could have asked to walk *with* her along the lane...Damn it!" But that was then, this was now, and he had a little more sense now than he had then. A very little.

The bird-less cuckoo clock said five until five, not literally aloud, but rather the clock's hands expressed themselves to Bernard with the same delicacy of a bellow through a blow horn. The very idea of being late and missing the opportunity of seeing Miss Kennari drenched Bernard in an instant sweat. A particularly uncomfortable little trickle ran down the small of his back into his butt cheeks. A part of him - the yearning, desperate part - wanted to close the shop early, but the sign in the window said Wimples would be open until 5:00 pm and unless it was a grumpling-sized emergency, he could not let down a hat buyer should one come along. He hoped one didn't come along.

He held his breath, his entire person rigid and motionless but for his sharp glances back and forth from the clock to the door. Four minutes left. Double-checking that everything was in order for the shop to be closed killed the third minute. With two minutes to go he was at the front window, peering up and down the length of the street and glad to see no approaching customers, regardless of how welcome the money might be. He turned towards the clock and stared unblinking as the final sixty seconds counted down.

"Eyeballs become very dry very quickly," he noted as tears rolled down his cheeks at the thirty second mark.

JINGLE! JINGLE! JINGLE! The doorbell startled him half out of his shoes and he fell back grasping at his heart fearing it had stopped from fright. A man and a woman waltzed in, clearly tourists by their "out-of-towner" appearance as the locals called it, an appearance humans would call "normal." They canvassed the entire shop with faces like Greek masks, the man clinging to hope, the woman expecting disappointment. They finally spotted Bernard picking himself up from between the homburgs and the panamas, which he'd literally been taken aback into due to the aforementioned startling.

"Hello, do you work here?" asked the man bending low to better meet Bernard's gaze and remaining bent even after Bernard stood fully upright.

"I--," Bernard attempted to jumpstart the sentence with a few more I's, then swallowed to get his vocal cords back in working order. "I am the proprietor."

"Excellent," declared the man, standing straight and tall in his straight and tall pin-stripped suit. Bernard noted, not for the first time, just how large they made these out-of-towners. "I was wondering if you had something for my wife." The equally tall but lankier woman leaned out just slightly from behind her husband and her bare shoulders gave Bernard the

impression that she was naked. His face burned a bright pink with
embarrassment in one instance and then went red in the second instance
with an overwhelming sense of indignation that someone would be so bold
as to walk into his shop without wearing a single stitch to speak of.
Bernard was about to throw the couple out of his store for indecent
exposure, but was spared buckets of embarrassment when the woman
stepped into full view and he could see that she wore quite a few stitches
actually, enough to make up a strapless sundress.

"Ah," said Bernard, gradually returning to a less heart-attacky
color.

"The thing is," the man went on, "we'll be out on the water all day
tomorrow and my sweetilydeets didn't bring a hat." It may not have
seemed it by the repetition of another noncommittal "ah," but Bernard had
the situation in hand now.

"Something, I believe, with a wide brim would be ideal," said the
man holding his hands out beside his head to indicate a rather wide brim
indeed.

"I'm afraid men's hats are all I carry, sir." The man and woman
sent chin-lifted scans over the tiny shop, his being investigative and hers
perfunctory. Both registered disappointed findings.

"Yes, I see." A broad chagrin draped itself from the man's
crisscross forehead to his drooping lip.

"I told you," whispered the woman as she turned her whole body
on him. If they weren't going to buy anything Bernard was quite ready for
them to leave, but the man gave a last gasp look about the place.

"Nothing even womanish?" he asked.

"Womanish men's hats, sir?" asked Bernard.

"You know the sort of thing…feathers, gay colors and all that
jazz?" The question had sincerely perplexed Bernard. He wasn't even sure
how to answer it, such an odd question never having been put to him
before.

"These are men's hats, sir," he finally said and wished with
clenched teeth in a tone slightly lower than under-his-breath that they
would "Go. The. Fuck. Away."

"Come on, Alfie, let's go," said the woman plucking at the man's
sleeve. Bernard's respect rose by leaps and bounds for this sensible woman
with the sound ideas.

"Just a sec," said the man smiling down at a trilby. "How do you
think I'd look in one of these?" he asked, twisting about to show his wife,
who didn't hear him over the jingling bell as she exited the shop. "Hm.

91

Thank you," he said to Bernard with a painful little smile as he dropped the trilby cockeyed on to a fedora and followed after the woman.

Bernard put the hat back in its place, hurried around behind the counter to ring up a "NO SALE!" on the cash register. There was no time to count the receipts, which added an ounce of comfort to the fact that there were no receipts to count. A quick flip of the sign from "Open" to "Closed" and he was off.

The lengthening rays of the afternoon sun flooded warm gold upon Main Street's captivatingly colored shops lining both sides of the cobble stone road. It blinded Bernard as it did just about every sunny day when he finally emerged after a long workday within the relatively dark confines of the haberdashery. He shielded his eyes and ducked around a corner as soon as possible, not only to save his sight, but also to avoid Main Street.

The problem with the old main drag was that between his shop and Thee Toffee Shoppee lay the lair of Nana James, an elderly person who may or may not have been one of his grandparents. He couldn't remember if James was a first or last name. Nor could he remember a time when Nana James didn't have a fuzzy moustache. He wasn't 100% comfortable calling her a she, as her inclusion within the fairer sex seemed dubious at best. He only referred to her as a she because he'd once heard someone else do it and it seemed the polite thing to do.

One thing he could be sure of Nana James was that her ever-vigilant eye would inevitably emerge from the always-unshuttered front window of her rank man-cave of an apartment above Chandler's Candlery and it would spot him strolling down the street. She'd then beckon him in, a beckoning that could not be refused, for like all old ladies she held and deftly wielded the power of small town gossip and its subsequent condemnation. "Did you hear about the hatter who refused to help his grandmother?" they would say. Once Nana James got him inside under the guise of performing some menial and unnecessary task that she claimed to be urgent even though it had remained uncompleted these many decades, she would torture him at her whim with tales so boring as to make accountants weep. If he wasn't being bored by her, he was getting beat up by her. But that will have to wait for another story, because Bernard was all too aware of how detrimentally delaying her tasks and tales would be to his current purpose.

"Her photo album admiring sessions, attic explorations or god knows what will have to wait!" he declared while jogging with a jiggle and a "crunch-crunch" crunching of pebbles that covered the back lane, praying all the while he wasn't too late to meet Miss Kennari. After the village tea shop's patio garden came the critical moment when he had to pass back over Main Street. He crossed his fingers, hoped whomever in this world was in charge of good timing was on his side, even said a Hail Mary for good measure and then rolled the dice, dashing across the road with his eyes closed, evoking the sage wisdom of children through out the ages, "if you can't see it, it can't harm you."

Either luck, coincidence or divinity was indeed on his side as he scurried up Franklin Street to safety and stopped in front of Thee Toffee Shoppee. And gods be praised, there she was! Through the window he could see the back of the schoolteacher at the counter making her purchase. He hastened inside perhaps a little too hastily, because he looked anxious standing there heaving in great gulps of air, his gasping lungs thrusting his concave chest in and out like a dilapidated set of bagpipes. He was indeed anxious and didn't need extra help looking the part, not when his clammy hands and sweaty brow were doing such a splendid job of it on their own. Complete composure may have been out of the question, but he did his best, mopping his brow and such. The only problem with mopping one's brow with equally sweaty hands is that the perspiration doesn't get wiped away so much as smeared around. It's just as well Bernard's eyes weren't in a good position to see his glistening, streaky forehead.

Miss Kennari was looking nicer than usual in a clean, ankle-length dress with a pattern of gigantic flowers and her straight, not-blond-but-actually-yellow hair free of tangles and paste. Perhaps that seems nothing special, but Bernard couldn't imagine anyone looking much nicer than she did, and truth be told, Miss Kennari didn't always look this nice. Usually she wore dowdy clothes at school, like muumuus and smocks in case she got caught up in a finger-painting accident or a particularly explosive nose blasting from one of her oft-ill students or any other of the hundred and one ways in which schoolteachers get mightily mussed. But on days when she would buy her candy she changed into her best clothes after the children had gone home and the danger had passed. Bernard didn't realize such an extra effort was being made. If he did, he would have suspected it was for Superintendent Nes, a relatively handsome, well-dressed man in a position of power, and that would have definitely put him off of Miss Kennari.

Bernard could see she'd already made her purchase, a strawberry drop from the shop-soiled jar, the same discount selection he always chose from as well. They were both people of modest means, both having fallen on hard times: his hats-only haberdashery had struggled as of late and she was a schoolteacher. Somehow their mutual poverty comforted him, an odd circumstance considering how money woes often provided nothing but cold comfort. Being no psychologist he couldn't exactly say why their equally poor financial footing set his mind more at ease, but he figured love was to blame, a safe bet when usually rational things like common sense go awry.

"Good afternoon Miss Kennari," said Bernard with a tip of his dented bowler.

"Very good afternoon, Mr. Wimple," she said. So very prettily said, thought Bernard before striking the thought from his mind to concentrate on the next few, absolutely important lines.

"You're looking ni--"

"Hello Bernie! What would you like?!" chimed in the all-too chirper tones of Pollip the candy store clerk, a middle-aged, pear-shaped woman dressed in a fuzzy, pink tracksuit with her hair in pigtails and generous dollops of make-up smeared about her face in an attempt to look 20-years younger. It had the opposite effect.

"Hello Pollip," said Bernard. He would've rather said, "My name is Bernard, not Bernie and please stop interrupting me, you painted nightmare you", but there was no point.

Pollip was a lost cause. While not the owner, she ran the store. Although, to say she "ran" might not be the right word. Perhaps saying she "walked the store" would be closer to the mark. Once finally in motion, Pollip could make a snail seem hasty. Bernard suspected her mother might have slept around with one of the local firemen. Her wit was not much quicker. Oh she could pop out a few words with vim and vigor, but often her ejaculations were mashed together in a monstrously unholy marriage of sinfully synthesized superlatives. For example, she might combine "surely" and "certainly" to get "surtainly!" or conjoin "marvelous" and "fantastic" to get "marvelastic!" It became apparent to Bernard that she developed this annoying tic from the song "'S Wonderful," a tune she could often be heard humming as she slothed about behind the counter. For that reason alone Bernard had a large bone to pick with Ira Gershwin. Anyhow, as you can see, by putting her in charge of the candy shop's daily operations, the owners of Thee Toffee Shoppee were seriously jeopardizing the welfare of their business. At this moment she was busy jeopardizing Bernard's love life.

"I would like one strawberry drop, please," requested Bernard.

"All out, Bernie!" She delivered the bad news as chipper as always without losing her ever-present silly grin.

"All out? But I…I, but…oh, very well," he said with perturbation. So focused was he on the woman he hoped still stood behind him waiting to conclude the conversation they'd started, that he couldn't think of the name of any other candies. He scanned the store for inspiration. While it may not have been as grand as a certain famous chocolate factory owned by a reclusive maniac and operated by little orange men, Spritzerville was proud of its toffee shop. They didn't carry every type of sweetmeat known to man, but what they did have they had in abundance. The brightly lit store was packed with glass jar after glass jar lining shelf upon shelf, all filled with any manner of stick candy, lengthy lines of red vines, long boys stacked like logs and candies that evoked nature, such as peppermint bark and many rock specimens, while strips of button candy dangled from cartwheel-sized rolls attached to the low-hanging rafters. This horde of rainbow colored sugary delectables surrounded him and yet he still could not come up with a single name for one of them. He focused on the shop-soiled jar with its busted, encrusted, and dusty treats, and there in the jar's rounded reflection Miss Kennari's face gleamed back at him.

"Those lips," he inadvertently blurted, his eyes shocked wide open by his own words.

"Lips?" a perplexed Pollip questioned and then burst out with an exceptionally enthusiastic "Absatively!" all while staring at him with one bright, gleaming eye while the other, lazy and droopy-lidded, floated independently at random. Her crisp, energetic replies no doubt duped many a first time patron with hopes of receiving prompt service. Such hopes were agonizingly dashed as she waddled to and fro absentmindedly forgetting to grab a bag, snagging the wrong sweet due to ocular difficulties or just flat out heading in the wrong direction. With her maneuverability and reaction time ranked well below village average, these trifling missteps turned into ponderous detours. Bernard felt a lifetime pass as he waited for a pair of wax lips he didn't even want.

"It's a shame they were all out of drops," came Miss Kennari's voice from behind, startling his innards.

"Ah, yes, quite a shame," he gurgled while dislodging his stomach from his throat.

"I feel awful for taking the last one. Would you like to share mine?" she asked with a cordial smile. Inexperience and nerves tied his tongue like a champion tongue twister working over an opponent with a vice, grips, and yards of pliable tongue.

"No. Ah, no thank you, that is," was all he could think to say.

Miss Kennari began speaking, but was drowned out by the boisterous bellow of Pollip finally returning with his lips, and so Bernard missed the first half of "Well, have a…" and only caught the later half, which was "…nice day."

"Yes, it is a very nice day indeed," he replied, taking the bagged wax lips and shoving the coin into Pollip without looking where it ended up. Through the ridiculous white noise of Pollip behind him he said, "A very nice day for a walk, if you would care to join me?" and couldn't believe he'd said it. The sound and the fury between his ears muddled her reply, so he never did know if she said yes or no, but he guessed it was a yes, because the next thing he knew the two of them were walking along the river together.

Bernard had mixed feelings about rivers, but on this day he thought he'd never seen a finer river than the one flowing alongside the two of them. Like a sparkly vampire, it positively twinkled in the twilight as well as from the stars within his eyes as it sucked and slurped away. His bland wax lips even tasted sweet, in a way. Sure, he felt a fool with them stuck in his mouth, but they did that magical thing called "breaking the ice." Planted in the mouth of Mr. Bernard Eloise Wimple, Miss Dimple Kennari found them comical. It made him think that perhaps allowing oneself to look ridiculous in moderate doses might have its value.

"Dimple?" he asked her, once they'd shifted to being on a first name basis.

"My father named me, because I have a dimple." Her explanation seemed incomplete to Bernard, who studied her face - chubby in the cheek department though not full-blown flabby - and saw nothing like what might be called a dimple. He guessed it was somewhere else on her body and then he guessed where most dimples are if they are not on the face. He wished he hadn't guessed at all, because thinking about Miss Kennari's derriere muddied up his end of the conversation just as it was beginning to flow along with the same ease as the river. He began floating adrift in words like aimless flotsam upon the water, no clue where it had been or where it was going. This fluid confusion felt akin to a dose of loose bowels. Not a very romantic analogy, but that's what was on Bernard's mind. When the conversation lulled or hopped on to a topic he was not familiar with, he went all butterfly-in-the-belly jittery.

When it came to butterflies, especially the social butterfly, Bernard was out of his depth. These days he was mostly happy to hang out in his own cocoon, which was not the case when he was a young jack-the-lad back in the day. "The day" didn't last long, perhaps a year round about when he was seven or eight. Not exactly prime time for courting the ladies. After a few subsequent attempts it all pretty much went down hill from there. The poor boy was not to blame. At some indeterminate point during the utterly critical early developmental stages of the romance regions of his brain, Bernard contracted Deveraux Deficiency, a.k.a. "the lack of love" and subsequently suffered a string of romantic missteps. For example, in his early teens, Bernard went through a "missed kiss" phase. When leaning in to plant a kiss he literally missed. His eyes would close too soon, his aim was off or the target would move. Any which way, the girl cut loose. Then there was the "Year of the Bad Joke." It would be cruel to tell the joke now, being that Bernard's grown up and learned from the mistakes of his silly youth. So it must suffice to say that during this unfortunate period in his life, Bernard went around trying to impress various girls he liked by telling a joke he thought was hilarious, but which was not. Jokes combining fisherman and magicians who do card tricks seldom are. Nope, not funny in the least. Also, there was an embarrassing episode in which he walked into class with his fly down and all the kids laughed at him, except for the girls who were too busy screaming. He made an apology to the girl he liked at the time, but that only made it worse, because she looked at him like he was crazy and said, "I don't care. I don't care about anything you do." Not only was it demoralizing, the incident traumatized Bernard right into a zipper-checking obsession that eventually led to him wearing only zipperless pantaloons, which attracted yet more ridicule.

Once he realized most of his attempts at pitching woo were ending in those sorts of sorry shenanigans, he gave up. Finding love seemed like a lost cause. This is not to say he didn't still long for love and admire the married, and he most certainly still had his own personal preferences when it came to women. In fact, he was what you might call a "leg man." He wouldn't have been opposed to dating a woman without legs, but he greatly preferred that they owned a pair. Miss Kennari had legs, he was fairly sure. She wore long skirts, so he wasn't 100% positive, but as she hopped down a short, uneven set of wooden steps along the riverbank, he caught an exciting glimpse of ankle, which tends to indicate leggedness.

Walking side by side – a pensive Bernard with his head down, a sprightly Miss Kennari with her head up – they'd gone quiet, in part, because Bernard wished to slip through Landmand's Grove undetected, which they did, but also because they seemed to have run the gauntlet of ready topics. Feeling the oppressive weight of the conversational lull, Bernard most dreadfully fell back on his old ways.

"Miss Kennari…I'm sorry, Dimple, may I ask you a question?"

"Of course, Bernard," she said with a smile that bolstered his courage.

"What did the fisherman say to the card magician?" Bernard asked his stale old joke with all eagerness and anticipation of Miss Kennari, whose moment of quizzical thought produced only a shrug. "Pick a cod, any cod!" he called out like a carny barker on the midway. Nope, still not funny…but wait. Miss Kennari tittered. It was barely audible at the start, but after some more tangible titters, she most definitely snorted.

"Oh! Excuse me," she said through her hand over a wave of giggles. As luck would have it for Bernard, Miss Kennari had an affinity for bad jokes. It was one of the reasons she'd become an elementary school teacher, a vocation that exposed her to a wealth of one-liners and sub-sophomoric slapstick.

Bernard's butterflies flew away and he relaxed enough to think beyond the very next thing coming out of his mouth, such as noticing that with the sun setting and the evening air chilling, Miss Kennari might be getting cold with only her frayed and holey knit sweater to keep her warm.

"It's a cool night. I imagine your apparel isn't enough to keep you warm," he said.

"Yesss," she said shivering. Bernard couldn't remember in the history of himself when he'd ever been so incisively intuitive in regards to a female, especially of the feminine persuasion. He was so pleased with himself that he forgot to offer her his coat. Instead, he daydreamed of a lengthy and potentially gratifying discussion they might have on the weather, with comments pertaining to the time of year and warmth of the day as opposed to the night. From there he thought he might discuss with her the thick, towering hedge of pink and violet sweet pea flowers filling the air with their perfume-from-the-past sensuous intoxication. With this wall of flowers now alongside them it would've been a natural progression, especially since it appeared they were causing Miss Kennari to have an allergic reaction. She dabbed at her red, watering eyes with a paint-stained handkerchief. All that would have been very nice indeed, thought Bernard, but instead something awful happened.

A monumental stench, like the den of a prolific dung beetle, who really excelled at his day job, struck them a vicious blow to their noses, wrinkling them up like compressed accordions. Being caught up in their - the word "date" sounds too strong, let's call it a "walk" - so, being caught up in their walk, they'd absentmindedly passed the sign that read: "Ye Olde Cesspit."

Ye Olde Cesspit was where the village piped its excrement, which was spit out here into an overflowing and ever-widening pool. In this feces-filled swamp there lived a creature called the Poop Baby. It sat before them wallowing in a particularly nasty puddle of muck gleefully munching on a fresh turd.

"Eee-gahlaump," went the happy gurgling swallow of the hairless, almost-human larvae-like oddity as brown as the waste it sat in waist-high. With a playful, slime-splattering slap at the surface, it was all too apparent that the Poop Baby delighted in its surroundings and took great pleasure in the sewerage refinement service it provided to the village.

I wouldn't suggest eating those mushrooms.

Bernard watched in stricken horror as it slurped down a three-fingered handful of some indescribably gross guck and then burped it back up again. Miss Kennari's face, a pure palette of green frozen in a state of revulsion, turned to Bernard in alarm, her panicky eyes going wide, white and wild as they searched for escape from this nightmare, seeking a tranquil haven of sight and smell that she might wretch upon in private. Without a word, she skedaddled, her skirt whipping about her two very real legs like a flag in a hurricane. Bernard trotted along the path after her halfway back to the village, calling her name once or twice before his breath gave out and she, sprinting like a gazelle set upon by lions late to lunch, put distance between them until finally disappearing into the gnarled apple trees of Landmand's Grove. He had no idea she was that fleet of foot, but as soon as the futility of the chase became apparent he slowed down until coming to a standstill, gazing at the point in which he had last seen her yellow hair and flowery dress unfurling.

"Never before has athletic prowess seemed so admirable and...lovely. Oh hello, what's this?" At his feet lay Miss Kennari's handkerchief. He picked it up, looked up the path after her with a forlorn hope and then proceeded at a leisurely stroll, kicking at the stones and pine cones in the path, finding no pleasure in the flowers, even forgetting his hunger and forgoing the fallen apples from the grove as he contemplated what went right during their walk before it all went so, oh-so wrong. "What went wrong was that that Poop Baby was ever born!" he spluttered out. A fair bit of damage control needed doing because of today, but it would be another week before he might "accidentally" bump into Miss Kennari again. At that rate, it seemed to him that it would take a lifetime to fix this mess.

Dinner that night tasted like nothing, the house was as lively as a morgue and time most definitely dragged its feet as he brooded over what he'd already dubbed The Catastrophe At The Cesspit.

"Does anything ever good come of a cesspit?!" The anger in his shaking voice must have been obvious, because Gaiety hopped on to his lap and tried to cheer him up.

"Burwurd! Grabe!" it croaked, trying to say, "Bernard is great!" in its odd little ribbit language, which Bernard understood as only a mother understands the garbled words of her marble-mouthed toddler.

"Thank you, but it's no use, my little friend," said Bernard, stroking its warty back, "I'm a born failure in the ways of love."

Try as he might to distract his thoughts with his favorite hobbies of an evening like hat reorganization and heartbeat counting, he just couldn't concentrate and found no pleasure in his usual leisurely pursuits. He hit the hay early that night. Upon waking the next morning he immediately remembered the day before and let slip a deflating groan as he rolled over and tried to fall back to sleep, if only to forget a little longer. When people talk of procrastination they usually refer to putting off a task, but there is such a thing as procrastinating for the purpose of putting off the plunge into an inevitable and dreadful emotional rollercoaster. However, unless you whack yourself hard in the head and cause a very specific sort of amnesia, there's no stopping this Dante's Inferno trek into the depths of the heart.

He got dressed without thought for his appearance, ate with no appetite, very nearly forgot to feed his toady, then went to work with little else on his mind but Miss Kennari. At the end of the workday he was in such an absentminded daze he could not have told you if he'd even served a single customer all that day.

"Single," sighed Bernard, "that's what I'll be the rest of my days..."

The hippie mice living in his walls were familiar enough with Bernard's ways to know the difference in his moods. They weren't always, let us say *aware*, but they could tell the difference between a bored absentmindedness and a distressed one. As he was going through the motions of closing up the shop, the mice sauntered into and slouched about the haberdashery.

"Not all is copacetic with captain capitalist, his heinous, King of Landlordia," said Daddy-o, a tall, skinny, pointy goateed mouse dressed in a black turtleneck, a black beret, and circular blue-tinted granny glasses. He was more of a beatnik, but he hung with the hippy crowd and was always the first to decry labels, even though he tended to use them a lot in reference to Bernard.

"What's got ya bummed, B?" asked Cheddar, a surfer dude through and through, from his bleached blonde doo to the very salty saltwater that soaked him to the bone. He and Bernard hadn't gotten along at first. In fact Bernard had tried to kill him. But that was water under the bridge and nothing a few joints wouldn't help forget. Now they had a casual chinwag with the friendly ease associated with a long acquaintanceship. Bernard relayed the bitter details of The Catastrophe At The Cesspit. Although it was funny from an outsider's perspective, the mice were kind enough to repress their laughter. And Daddy-o, mistakenly thinking he was doing Bernard a further kindness, related the following news.

101

"You won't have to worry about that chicky-baby much longer. She's on the outs, man."

"What?" asked Bernard, not understanding what the mouse said, but not liking the sound of it.

"Yeah man, she'll be splitsville before ya know it."

"She'll be in Spritzerville?"

"*Splitsville*, man! Gone-zo, sayonara, arrivederci, bye bye. Capisce?"

"Oh…Oh no! What do you mean? I mean, why is she splitsville?"

"Why? Why brother she's got no students ta teach, that's why. No students, no teacher gig, ya dig?"

"Yes, yes, I dig completely. Thank you. Thank you very much," said a very concerned Bernard. Not a man who'd normally trust a bunch of stoned mice, he nonetheless suspected their information to be solid. Every house, hovel, shop, factory, bank, windmill, you name it, they've squatted it, and while crashing at these pads, along with the munchables, they'd devour the local gossip. This particular little tidbit dropped on Bernard like a ton of bric-a-brac. The rest of the day he spent contemplating the fairness this world had to offer. In the end he concluded it had none. Here he was, middle-aged with very little prospect of ever finding love and now the one chance he'd had in ages was slipping away. He was not a man of great romance. He would never woo a lady with his charm, good looks, animal magnetism or properly placed words in conversational situations. But did he not deserve to love and be loved in return, he asked himself.

"Perhaps not."

As happens when it seems all hope of love is lost, everything he saw on his way home reminded him of her: the delicious-as-candy looking gingerbread work decorating the tea shop's façade; the canary perched in a cage hanging on Miss Carolina Rhoads' porch; the legs on a table in the furniture store window. Everything reflected back as Miss Kennari, so that night he sat at home alone in the dark hoping that if he couldn't see anything at all maybe he might forget about her. It didn't work, not even when he shut his eyes. Instead, all of his long-term remembrances of Miss Kennari inundated his thoughts and played upon the dark screen of his closed eyelids. A lonesome depression as sad as Terry Bradshaw performing "The Last Word in Lonesome is Me" crept upon him. If he had the tools and wherewithal, he could have created the most melodramatic poem in history and would have been heralded the world over as a poetic genius by melancholic teenagers everywhere. But that golden opportunity passed by without him even realizing it, and frankly that's for the best.

By the next night, having spent the day heaping on the misery in his mind and driving himself to despair, Bernard was looking to drown his sorrows once and for all. The Ol' Drinking Well was the place to do it. Built ages ago in Ticking Square, the well was a round and waist-high stone structure topped off with a stout wooden roof and pulley that held a sturdy rope with a barrel-sized bucket tied to one end.

Bernard dragged his feet and his heart down to the square after dark. Crank, a partially brawny pulleyman with one enormously muscular arm, slept in a chair leaning back against the well with his folded arms and chin resting on his chest, which rose and fell with a meaty snort-and-wheeze repetition. Without waking him, Bernard stepped up to the well and leaned over the edge, looking down into a dark and empty void to the unseen waterless, solid rock bottom below, enough of a drop to end it all if a person went headfirst.

"There's nothing for it," said Bernard with regretful resignation. He plucked up the courage and cleared his throat.

"Burrrubhumhum...at your service, at your service...Mr. Wimple?" said the pulleyman jumping up from his chair and rubbing his eyes clear.

"Hello, Crank. Sorry to wake you," said Bernard handing the man two copper coins.

"Roundtrip then, Mr. Wimple?" Crank couldn't help chuckling at his own little joke. The joke being that a ride in the bucket was the only way up and down the well, so it was always a round-trip for everyone. Bernard tried his best to smile as he crawled into the bucket, but the thing below his nose would've looked more like a smile if he'd been upside down. Crank didn't seem to notice and was still chuckling as he turned the crank with his one powerful arm, lowering Bernard into the well in a rapid but controlled descent. Touching down with a gentle tap upon the ground, Bernard climbed out of the bucket, snagged his foot on the rope, did a hop-step trip and hit his head on the unseen pulleyman's bell, after which the bucket instantly whooshed back up the shaft.

"Heeey," came Crank's ticked-off perplexity echoing back down the shaft a moment later.

Bernard peered into the darkness of the Ol' Drinking Well. Having once been a water well, there were minor unpleasantnesses, such as the occasional damp caused by leaking cracks in the walls and the drafts whipping up from the cavern whenever the door to the subterranean river were opened, but besides that it was as cozy a spot as one could hope for in which to get their drink on. Being many feet underground and thus windowless, it was solely and only very dimly lit by yellowing light fixtures suspended from the low ceiling by chains, but it was a warm, golden glow that was cast upon the walls where hung various plaques, trophies, and news clippings, all of local importance. Above a jukebox was a chalkboard that always said "Happy New Year!" In the middle of the room amongst the tables and chairs was a pig carved into one of the wooden support columns standing on its hind legs and holding up a tray with its front legs. Crowded along the bar were the comfortably cushioned barstools with wrought iron backs that the regulars coveted. A few bums were already planted in them. A wine rack built into the wall behind the bar housed basic and boring reds and whites, but there also could be found the odd pineapple wine or occasionally the highly illegal baby moose wine. The more popular doppelberry ale with its dual personality and the heady hydra milkshake stout were available on tap with the pull of the fancy pump handles, but even they couldn't top the taste of the Well's own, matchless Honeybunny Mead (made from real honeybunnies!) served special in ornate pewter mugs.

"A beer, Bernard?" called out the round-nosed, curly-haired bartender mopping up a puddle forming at one end of the bar. By "beer" he meant Bernard's usual root beer.

"Something a bit stronger I think this time, Simon," said Bernard.

"A hard root beer then?" said Simon. Simon was not the bartender's real name. It was Salmon. His parents were Alaskan fishermen and a little kooky. When he moved to Spritzerville and started working at the Well, the first person to ask him his name mistook it for Simon and Salmon was quite happy to live with the mistake.

"Make it a rum punch, please," said Bernard as he pulled up a stool, missing the bartender's raised eyebrow. He needed a stronger drink than his usual, something potent to wash away his sorrows. But any ideas he had of doing this drowning-of-distress alone were squelched upon the arrival of his friendly acquaintances, the philosophizing Ludwig and the inquisitive Felix, those intellectually lively Dawdlekat brothers. Half a dozen moments later and half into his drink, Bernard was already half in the bag. His solo introspection had morphed into more of a community forum, especially as other folks -also mere acquaintances - packed in tight around him to volunteer their opinions on the slightly slurred conversation into which he poured out all his rotting guts.

"Love is the devil," said Ludwig. "The very devil!"

"True, true," agreed the others.

"So there's nothing for it then? She's gone?" asked Felix.

"Shizz gone...gone," said a drowsy-eyed, floppy-headed Bernard. "An' all I hab...have to...ya know, to...Wuz tha' fing ya do when ya don't furget?"

"Remember?" offered Felix.

"Right! An' all I hab ta rememble her by is this." He pulled Miss Kennari's handkerchief out of his pocket and waved it in his friend's faces. "Fawoof! That stinks! Get it out of here!" they hollered, throwing their hands up as if to ward off a swarm of very stinky bees.

"Whadaya mean?" Bernard sniffed it and jerked his head like he'd been tweaked on the nose. Sure enough, it smelt like poo. His face went horribly sour and vengeful as he roared, "Damn tha Poof Baybay!" His vehemence shocked the others. They'd never seen Bernard in such a raging fury, like a wild beast unleashed. Granted, the beast may have been akin to a hedgehog, but a wild one nonetheless. "Tha' good fur nothin'," he cursed.

If we could just stop Bernard right there for one moment. Calling the Poop Baby "Tha' good fur nothin'!" besides being atrocious grammar, is a flat-out unfair character besmirchment. It has been clearly shown that the Poop Baby provided a very important service to the community via sewerage processing. Okay, let's return to Bernard's drunken rant.

"Probly dun't hev a edgykayshun an' cudn't git a bettah job anywho, the soddin' sod." BINGO! Those incomprehensible words flicked on the ol' idea light bulb within his head. His eyes widened and blinked as if the flash in his brain had gone off in his face. Dazed and amazed, he silently swayed on his stool and worried those around him that he might fall off backward. "Tha's it," he said as if in a trance. "Somebody take thiz down." There was no pen, no paper, or anything to take anything down with and no one made a move to do so anyhow, they were too riveted to Bernard and what might come out of his mouth next. What came out of his mouth was slow, deliberate and drenched in the devious. "I'mma git the Poob Baybay."

"Bernard, my man, is that really the logical next step? Is it even moral to *git* a baby?" posited Ludwig, looking into Bernard's eyes, concerned for his state of mind.

"No, you mis...mis-git me," said Bernard with a knitted brow that came undone as he went on. "I'mma git tha' baybay edgy-kated!" It seemed incredible to the audience huddled around Bernard that in his highly inebriated state, he had come up with a sound plan to save the schoolteacher's job and his chances at love.

"Hey, who says ya can't think straight when you're on the sauce?" interjected Simon the bartender.

After that the party really got started. Drinks disappeared fast and so did Bernard's meager savings, but he didn't care. In his irrepressibly good mood, he would've spent all the world's money right then. For whatever part it played in helping him arrive at the answer he so desperately sought, he felt he owed the Ol' Drinking Well a great debt and would've paid anything if it meant a chance to be with Miss Kennari. Bernard was a live music purest, but that night he felt an overwhelming need for a "kicking tune," as he'd once heard it said. Something to cook the blood and end the night on a real high note was called for, so he made an exception and popped a coin into the jukebox, selecting Benny Goodman's version of the "Beer Barrel Polka." However, some "punk kid," as Simon the bartender referred to them as, had replaced that song with The Black Keys "Tighten Up."

"What the deuce?!" cried the bartender, dropping his drop-cloth in surprise. Bernard dismissed the exclamation with a wave that said "Let it ride, brotha." And that's just what Bernard did. As the blaring rock music blasted through the Well, he pulled down his rumpled waistcoat, inadvertently set his bowler at a jaunty angle while trying to straighten it, drunkenly strode with an unintentionally hip swagger across the room, spun a 360 around a chair he mistakenly thought had jumped out in front of him, finally made it to the bar where he downed the last of his drink, bid his acquaintances an "Adieu!" with an extravagant wave, strut toward the

exit in a less-than-straight line, taking his eye off where he was headed to flare out his moustache so that it twisted with magnificent twirls, and then fell headfirst into the bucket, his heel hitting the bell that woke up Crank, who pulled Bernard up the shaft with his legs dangling out of the top of the bucket and his companions cheering him on all the way.

At least he didn't kick the bucket...

The next morning was a rough one to wake up to. However, Bernard recovered in half the time it might have taken, being buoyed as he was by the recollection of his scheme. As schemes hatched up in a bar on a drunken bender go, this one didn't seem too flawed with beer-soaked logic in the light of day.

"We'll see how it looks when we put it to the test," he said after brushing his almost nonexistent hair and combing his teeth. No, he wasn't still drunk, but in the best way possible, his mind remained intoxicated with the hope of his plans.

The test came a few days later when Bernard managed to meet up with the schoolteacher again. Although she was not in a terribly good mood, he convinced her to go for a walk, a walk that could be said in some ways to have gone even worse than The Catastrophe At The Cesspit. In and of itself the walk was fine and, more importantly, fecal free, however the discussion was nothing but depressing. Miss Kennari disclosed her difficult situation, revealing the terrible truth from her own lips that she had had only one student left whose parents had been planning to send the child away to Winston Smith Academy, where their proud motto was "We'll keep a good eye on your child."

"And now they've gone and done it!" she sobbed. "I'm a student-less teacher! When Superintendent Nes arrives next week I'll be out of work and I'll have to move away to find a job at another school someplace else, if I'm lucky."

He'd never seen her cry before and the sight of her tears were like bee stings to his heart. The desire overcame him to, "do whatever people do to other people in these situations." To comfort her would've been a good start, but he didn't know how, so he just stood beside her feeling lame and at a loss. Add to that his smile. So happy and confident had he been going into this, that he'd started out with a big grin from ear to ear. Miss Kennari's unexpected emotional collapse caught him off guard, and so his insipid smile mingled with concern to create a fairly grotesque mask-like face, the sort of thing best worn only on Halloween. If Bernard's face was a storefront façade, the sign in the window would say, "Get your jolly horror here!" Anyone in the schoolteacher's position would understandably take it for ridicule, which is never appreciated, especially not at a time like this.

The circumstances were too much for him. He turned away, glancing everywhere around him but at Miss Kennari, who looked at him for the first time since her weeping had begun and saw nothing of his "jolly horror" mask, only the back of his head as he admired a rotted, less than admirable apple tree stump. Neither of them realized they'd stopped walking. No words passed between them, just the wind above the silence.

"I'm sorry about all the fuss I've made about me and my problems. I'm not very good company I'm afraid. I'm going to go." She turned and headed back. Bernard stood utterly stunned, only able to think about how amazingly wrong it all had gone.

"I can help. Come with me." The soft, but steady words slid out of him of their own volition. It might've been the wind who spoke them for all the effort with which they left his lips, sounding to him as defenseless and naked as if he'd said, "I love you."

"Where?" she asked, turning back to him with a twinkle of optimism returning to her eyes that spoke of a willingness to be led by him in the hope of finding an all but impossible answer. Whether it was out of her own desperation or an intangible quality in this balding, round-headed haberdasher, she couldn't put her finger on it yet, but something told her she could do worse than to place her faith in the hands of Bernard Eloise Wimple. However, even the most desperate among us have our limits.

"Oh hell no!" she bellowed as Bernard led her down to the high hedge of sweet peas just before the cesspit. She backed away like an animal being led to slaughter, glancing this way and that with frightened eyes seeking escape. "I'm not going back there!"

"You must trust me. I want to show you something. Please." Cajole all he might, Miss Kennari would have none of it.

"Don't you remember what happened last time? I'm feeling ill just thinking about it." Already she'd turned an unhealthy off-white.

"Here," said Bernard, taking from his waistcoat her handkerchief, cleaned and neatly folded. "Hold this up to your nose and…" he said, stepping over to the hedge and grabbing a handful of fragrant flowers, "…and hold these up to your nose too. Is that better?"

She felt a bit silly shoving a cloth and flowers in her own face and already her eyes were watering, but even so, it had been a while since any male over the age of six had done her such a kindness, misguided or not, and she soon forgot everything else, everything but Bernard.

"I have a plan to save your job," he said. He had no idea what she was thinking and maybe never would, not being a perceptive man when it came to these matters, but he saw her reddening eyes smile back at him just over the hanky and flowers and he knew what that meant.

"Okay, brace yourself. Here we are, the answer to all your problems!" he said, somewhat regretting the hyperbole, but soldiering on nonetheless, spreading his arms wide showmanship-style as they rounded the end of the hedge and came into full view of the cesspit. Miss Kennari's eyes stopped smiling. At best it could be said she was mildly flummoxed. Clearly she expected more. Her disappointment didn't phase Bernard's excitement in the least. In fine dramatic fashion with a relatively deep, carrying voice (almost a baritone, though nowhere near the Barry White tone he was going for) he declared, "May I reintroduce you to...the Poop Baby, the relief to your worrying condition!"

"I don't get it. Is this a joke?" There was an edge of irritation in her words that told Bernard he was losing his audience fast, so he launched into the explanation of his game plan and, by the time he was done, Miss Kennari's demeanor went from dubious to downright horrified.

"You want to bring that...that, no doubt lovely child, into the schoolhouse?"

"After a good scrubbing, yes."

"After a very good scrubbing with something toxic, perhaps."

"That's the spirit!"

"You honestly believe it can be done?"

"Of course! It won't take anything more than a little spit and polish, maybe a little elbow grease."

"Oh I'd leave out the grease."

"Very well then, but I guarantee to have one student ready, clean and awaiting your teachings at the start of the school week! We'll save your job if it's the last thing we do!" As against the plan as she was, she found his irrepressible determination infectious.

"Okay then," she said brightening up more and more as the idea took hold of her. "I have a student! Oh Bernard, thank you!" She gave one of his arms a squeeze. Bernard became acutely aware of how close she was standing to him and he thought she might even kiss him, a frightening and frighteningly exciting prospect. In the end the arm squeeze and a lovely smile beaming into his own ludicrous grin was all he got, but he was grateful for it. Besides, that was about as much excitement as his unaccustomed heart could handle.

Right away it became all too apparent to Bernard that revealing his plan and getting Miss Kennari onboard with it was actually the easy part. When he came back the following day, he realized he had no strategy yet to lure the Poop Baby away from its beloved cesspit. At first he tried coaxing it out with sweet words. He might as well have been painting the Invisible Man's portrait for all the good it did. Next he brought candied treats as enticement. That didn't work. He considered renting a van, driving right up to the cesspit, catching the Poop Baby unawares and tossing it into the back.

"Yeah, kidnapping-style," he said in a moment of triumph that was soon doused by a moment of reflection. "Oh wait, that would be considered kidnapping." Besides being too expensive and too illegal, there was also something all too creepy about it, not to mention vaguely familiar now that he gave it the twice over. Who was that man with the huge moustache and sunglasses he was just now recalling from his past? His concentration snapped at the sound of a juicy sputtering erupting from the sewerage pipe and a gleeful cheer from the bobbly, bulbous-headed, dopey-eyed Poop Baby.

"He sure loves his poo. What a simple soul. Hm, is it a he or is it a she?" While breezing through these airy thoughts, the 99.9% of his brain Bernard wasn't using plucked out the pertinent information he should have been focusing on and formed it into an answer, an answer his gray matter had to dangle in front of him for a while before the "Eureka!" moment arrived.

Putting a scoopful of the cesspit muck into a zip-lock baggy, Bernard carefully waved it in front of the Poop Baby's eager face, trying to tempt it away from its most cherished cesspit. Like a Slow Loris greedily grabbing for a single piece of fruit held by another Slow Loris - even though it was sitting in front of a whole bowl full of fruit - the Poop Baby crawled from the pool of unspeakable liquids and chunks, trailing a brown streak of slime behind it as it crawled all the way back to Bernard's cottage, or to be more precise, his backyard.

For as long as the daylight held out and for much of his free time over the next few days, Bernard hosed, soaped and scrubbed the Poop Baby. When finished he would stop for a break, take a look at his handiwork and start the whole process over again…and again…and again. He tried scraping and sanitizing. Nothing worked. The Poop Baby appeared to be soiled to the bone. Bernard did his best. It still glistened like wet fudge and smelled like an outhouse, but at least the largest chunks and the slipperiest slime came off and the stench smelled slightly less stinky.

Whether that was good enough would have to be seen, because before he knew it the start of the school week arrived. As promised, he had the Poop Baby at the schoolhouse ready for its first lesson.

"I don't know about this," an apprehensive-looking Miss Kennari said through her handkerchief.

"I have every confidence in the world of your skills of a teacher!" He wished her well and promised to come by at the end of the week to see how things had gone. The rest he had to leave in her capable hands so he could get back to work to drum up business in order to afford the extra cost of putting a child through school. With all this cleaning of poo and tiring slew of extra work, he was starting to feel like an actual parent. Lucky for Bernard though, unlike putting a normal child through school, the Poop Baby was relatively inexpensive. It didn't require books at this early stage, it didn't wear clothes, and food did not need to be purchased, for disgusting reasons already detailed.

The following week was almost entirely fantastic. No, sales did not improve and nothing happened that might give him hope that any were creeping around the corner about to spring their wealth upon him. The days were as uneventful as ever. Yet somehow they lacked boredom. There was excitement, possibility, the making of future plans, and many similar et ceteras! The only drawback was the yearning. Waiting while the week passed was excruciating. When not wrapped in elation, he was going right out of his mind thinking, worrying, and waiting, so much so that in an effort to ease his own suffering he made a terrible lapse in judgment, committing an act of murder. Willfully and without just cause, Mr. Bernard Eloise Wimple killed time.

Time is the orderly, irrevocable passing of our lives. By killing time, we kill life. Instead of being productive and utilizing his time to improve his mind, exercise his flabby body, make new friends, spend quality time with his pet toady or something quite practical like turning his unkempt backyard into a pleasant garden as he'd promed himself he would do for ages now, Bernard wasted the time staring out the window, twiddling his thumbs, glancing up at clocks irrationally hoping they'd move faster and just flat out wishing the time away, and by doing so with malice aforethought, Bernard was guilty of nothing less than first degree murder.

After leaving poor, old time bleeding in the street, Bernard didn't even glance back in his rearview mirror as he sped away - metaphorically speaking, as he had no automobile - in heart-pounded anticipation on his way to Spritzerville's old, one room schoolhouse with its high steeple and bell visible from just about anywhere in the village. As he arrived, Superintendent Nes burst from the front door with a horrid scowl and his fingers pinching his nose. Bernard feared the worst as he entered the school.

"Bernard," called out Miss Kennari. "Good news. Superintendent Nes isn't closing down the school!" She had her handkerchief tied around her face bandit-style, so it was hard to tell, he thought she appeared to be happy. "He wasn't impressed with the smell of the student, in fact he assumed the plumbing had backed up when he first got here, but he couldn't deny that PB, that's what I call it now, that PB is a real live student, so I can keep my job!"

"That is the best news ever!" Bernard's heart had never felt lighter. It rose so high in his chest that he quickly closed his mouth for fear it might pop out.

"There's also some bad news," she said and it was plain as day even from behind the bandit mask just how bad this bad news was. "The neighbors are complaining, not just about the smell, although I get plenty of those complaints, but if you believe it, the people of Dalsem's Crick over nearish to the cesspit, ya know? They're upset. They want their Baby back."

"They want their Baby back?"

"Yes. The mayor said, 'I want my Baby back' and he kept repeating 'Baby back' and then his wife said something about being chilly, but it was a warm, sunny day, so I don't know, but I think it has something to do with the sewerage backing up."

"Bah, it's high time we had a proper crap factory," declared Bernard, mounting his fists upon his hips in an outwardly decisive appearing stance.

"You mean *treatment plant*?"

"Is that what they're calling them these days? Well then, yes, one of those is in order, and a long time coming, too," he concluded with a resounding thump of his fist on the sticky top of a desk.

"But there's an even worse problem," said Miss Kennari. "Apart from PB getting, pardon me, fecal matter all over the school, books, walls, door handles, and that desk you just touched, he or she or whatever it is, just isn't…and this is going to sound harsh, but PB just isn't smart, not in the least. I can't teach it anything."

"Pish posh," Bernard retorted, scraping the muck off his hand on to another desk.

"No, it's true!" She led him to a tall cabinet in a corner and pulled from behind it several large sheets of paper. "I hid these from Superintendent Nes. They're PB's finger paintings." She flipped them over. If they were paintings, the only paint used was brown, and the subject was anyone's guess.

"Is it…," began Bernard, backing away from the stench and trying to play it off as if he were admiring it as if it were a Monet, "…is it a rain cloud?" Assessing the artistic merits of page after page of essentially the same single, dark, roundish splotch required in Bernard a good deal of polite optimism and what is known as "BSing."

"If they're anything, I mean *anything* at all, they must be the cesspit," she said, shrugging her shoulders in resignation.

"The Poo--er rather--PB will improve. I know you have it in you," he said.

"Thank you, Bernard. That's kind of you, but I've tried. I have, really. We've worked on letters and simple addition, but all it wants to do is spend all its time in the bathroom," she lowered her voice, "especially after I go, if you get my drift." She turned a touch red. "And you should see the disappointment on its face if I flush. It's so sad." She hung her head, dropped the paintings on her desk and slumped down in her chair. "I think we both have to be honest, PB wasn't meant for the world of higher education. It's not for everyone. Useless you've got another brilliant idea up your sleeve, I think it's time we set PB free. It needs to go back to the cesspit. He or she is a lovely…whatever it is, but it's sad to see how much it misses its muck."

Try as he might, and he did, Bernard could think of no solution and found no more valid arguments to refute hers, having exhausted every point of view from all angles. He stood there and she sat there, both quietly mulling it all over until arriving at the same inevitable conclusion and simultaneously letting out a long, sorrowful sigh.

"Well, that is very bad news indeed," said Bernard. There was nothing of worth left to say, only the incidentals that are said in the moment and forgotten in the next. Once those were out of the way, Bernard walked out to the fenced-in playground behind the school to a pint-sized, plastic playhouse, the Poop Baby's abode for the past week. The poor little thing looked as wretched as Miss Kennari made it out to be. It had lost some of its dark chocolate hue and its stench didn't curl Bernard's nose hairs as it once did.

"Come on," said Bernard, but it wouldn't come. It just sat there all pooped out. No amount of coaxing would make it come with him. Heading inside to grab something to wrap it in so he could carry it back to its home, Bernard stopped at the backdoor, turned and - looking around to make sure no one heard him – put his lips together and blew out a long, rippling fart noise. The Poop Baby perked up and toddled right up to him. From that point on it was clear that it would take only a mere matter of some minor personal embarrassment noise-wise on Bernard's part to lead the Poop Baby back to its home.

Back inside he stopped to say goodbye to Miss Kennari.

"I can't teach PB and I can't teach without PB. What can I do, Bernard? What can I do? Looks like this is it," she said, her mouth twisting about as she fought to steady the last words. She turned away from him and walked to the front door to show him out. She stopped with her hand on the knob and took a deep breath. "It's lovely what you tried to do for me. Truly. I really do appreciate it, but unless you have another plan, I'm afraid by next week, I'll be out of a job. They'll shutdown the school and I'll have to look elsewhere for work." He knew it was coming, but actually hearing it said hit Bernard harder than he expected and it must've shown. "It's kind of you to be so concerned," she said as a tear formed in the corner of her eye. She wiped it away, then leaned in and gave him quite possibly the quickest peck on the cheek in recorded history. To Bernard it was like a quick flash of heaven, a place it seemed he was doomed to never see again. "I've enjoyed our time to together as short as it was and I appreciate all you've done for me, but I'll be okay. I've applied to another position in Wilson."

"I don't even know where that is," said Bernard, his voice low and sullen.

"I don't know exactly either. I hear it's a few hundred miles away." As she said this, Bernard tried his best to subdue the excruciating rending of his innards. Even if the place were only a hundred miles away, it was as good as on the moon for all the traveling he ever did. "The pay isn't great, but they're in desperate need of teachers. So see," she gave his hand a little 'cheer up' shake, "I'll be okay. I promise I will."

Bernard wondered to himself, "Yes, but will I?"

114

A very dull day dawned and died just like the one before it, and Bernard Wimple feared, so would go the following day. He'd opened his shop on time, as always, and almost no customers came in, as always. Was he wasting his life away, standing behind the counter day after day leaning heavily upon it with his lulling head supported by a fist or two under his chin, he wondered that afternoon as he stood behind the counter leaning heavily upon it with his lulling head supported by a fist under his chin.

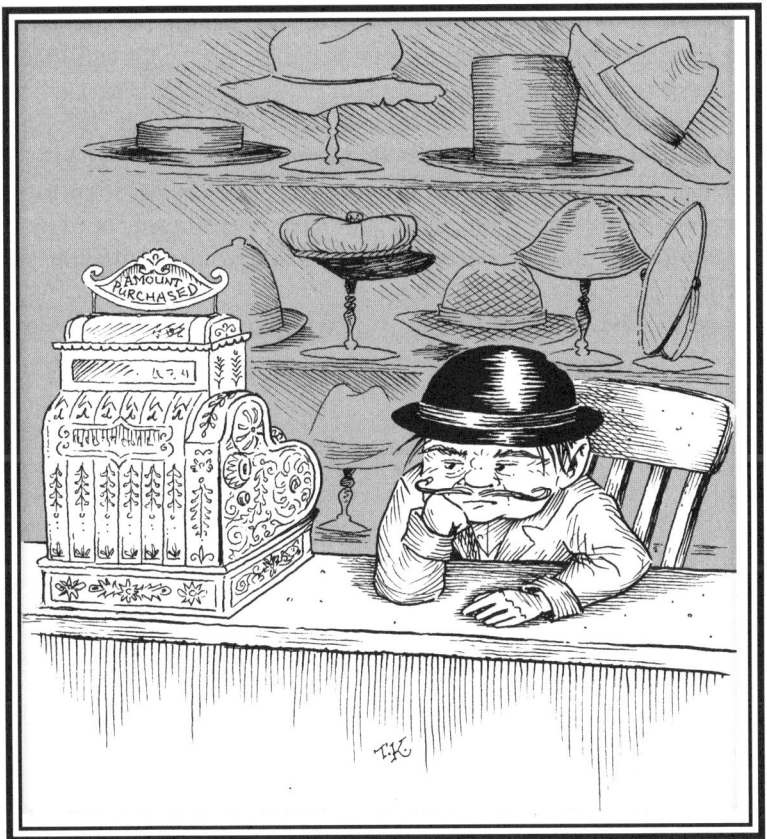

A very bored Bernard

Through his front window he watched with drowsy eyes the dangerously immense and red-faced Mr. Francis, struggling with laborious steps along the sidewalk across the street, suddenly clutch at his left arm, fall to his knees and collapse upon the pavement. A few good Samaritans eventually got him to his feet and he waddled off not looking much worse for wear. Bernard sighed.

"Nothing interesting ever happens," he said, propping a second fist under his chin. The day wore on and as it did his mind turned slowly about pondering upon the suckitude of his work and love lives, when approximately two minutes to closing time a strong desire to do something about it struck Bernard.

"When life hands you lemons, hand them right back!" he declared in a clear and carrying voice, while standing erect behind his counter with his meager chest puffed out defying ennui and giving the air before him a very stern glare just in case any ennui still lingered about. Life had been a little too lemony of late in his opinion. He resolved to do something about that and the resolution was punctuated by the birdless cuckoo clock announcing closing time, which instantly dissolved his resolution. Hunger and the comfort of home set in. That night he ate a plain supper of boiled toast, went to bed, got up the next day and did the whole damn thing all over again.

116

The Cold Old Couple

A very dull day dawned and died just like the one before it, and Bernard Wimple feared, so would go the following day. He'd opened his shop on time, as always, and almost no customers came in, as always. Was he wasting his life away, standing behind the counter day after day leaning heavily upon it with his lulling head supported by a fist or two under his chin, he wondered that afternoon as he stood behind the counter leaning heavily upon it with his lulling head supported by a fist under his chin.

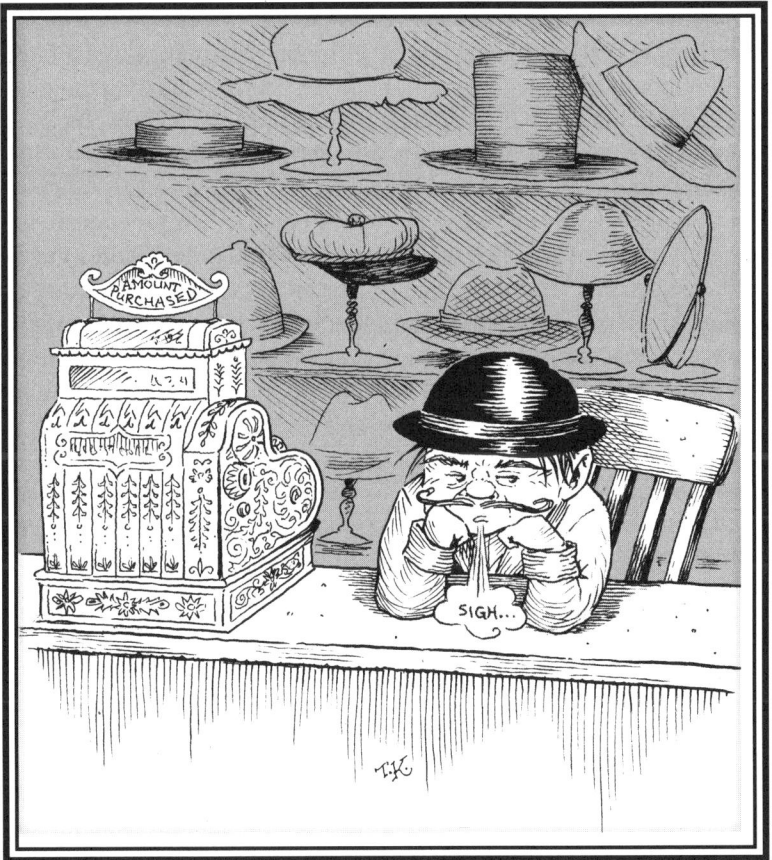

A very very bored Bernard

Through his front window he watched with drowsy eyes the dangerously immense and red-faced Mr. Francis, struggling with laborious steps along the sidewalk across the street, suddenly clutch at his left arm, fall to his knees and collapse upon the pavement. A few good Samaritans eventually got him to his feet and he waddled off not looking much worse for wear. Bernard sighed.

"Nothing interesting ever happens," he said, propping a second fist under his chin. The day wore on and as it did his mind turned slowly about pondering upon the suckitude of his work and love lives, when approximately two minutes to closing time a strong desire to do something about it struck Bernard.

"When life hands you lemons, hand them right back!" he declared in a clear and carrying voice, while standing erect behind his counter with his meager chest puffed out defying ennui and giving the air before him a very stern glare just in case any ennui still lingered about. Life had been a little too lemony of late in his opinion. He resolved to do something about that and the resolution was punctuated by the birdless cuckoo clock announcing closing time, which instantly dissolved his resolution. He went about the business of closing up his business for the day.

"No!" he shouted. "This simply will not do!" All too aware of life's suckitude, Bernard Wimple knew it was high time he did something about it, specifically regarding its love aspect. Previous plans to that end had come up short, such as his effort to woo Miss Dimple Kennari, the local schoolteacher, by saving her job. The scheme he hatched of turning a filth-strewn ragamuffin into an ad hoc student inevitably failed, putting the waif and the schoolteacher back in the shit, literally and figuratively, so something else had to be done to save her job and, more to the point in Bernard's eyes, to keep her in town. Being a slow woo-pitcher, he needed a tremendous amount of time to court her in his own awkward and restrained fashion, though he saw it as courteous and gentlemanly. In any event, he had to come up with another plan to keep her employed at the Spritzerville school and this was not proving easy.

"How to get it done?" "What else can I possibly do?" "Why do fools fall in love?" These were the machinations matriculating through the machinery of his mind as he locked up his shop that day. Then tinkle-dinkle chimes, reminiscent of a tone and tune deeply buried in his past, floated down Main Street striking Bernard in the earholes, lathering up his taste buds and yanking him back into the here and now. Rolling up the street at a pace that would make a turtle hoot in derision came an ice cream truck. It shone bright with its bottom half newly painted pink, the top half white. On the roof above the driver's cab perched a gramophone horn from which the twinkling tune emanated. All the wonderful dairy sweets and iced treats the truck sold were stenciled in brilliant colors around the sliding glass window from which the sugary delectables were dispensed. Bernard couldn't remember having seen an ice cream truck since he was an awfully young man. Even so, he certainly remembered the exhilarating thrill at the sound of the truck's tune, the mouthwatering anticipation, nagging his parents for money, the unstoppable jig he'd do while waiting on the sidewalk, and once getting so excited he wet himself.

"If ya keep that up the kids at school will call ya Mr. Peebody," his father insisted in an effort to frighten little Bernard out of ever doing it again. Being an impressionable youngster, he took it to heart and contained his excitement, which can tend to make a person rather colorless if taken to the extreme. However, at the time, the advice seemed sound, especially since there was a girl at school he wanted to impress and he knew it would be tough to do with soiled trousers. He'd once tried to lay on the charm by buying her an ice cream cone, but by the time he got to the girl's house on that sweltering day the ice cream had completely melted. Not even the cone resembled a cone, so much as a tired bit of soggy cardboard draped over his hand.

"Today's not half as hot as then. One could purchase an iced cream cone and transport it to a certain young woman not just a few blocks down the street afore it melts away. Brilliant! I'll buy two iced creams and share one with Miss Kennari. One might even call it a date, and a most perfect date that would make!"

As the truck neared he saw through the wide plate glass windshield the driver dressed smartly in starched white shirt and a pilotka, or as close to one as a pointy paper hat can be. A fear that he had no money on him seized Bernard. He tore through his pockets for coins only to find his keys. Fiddling with them furiously, he finally popped open the door to his haberdashery, ran inside, pried open the cash register and scooped up the three coins within. He thought about going to the safe.

"There's no time for the safe!" he declared and then remembered, "There is no safe!" After a long period of having nothing to put in it, he'd had to sell it.

Back out in the street, Bernard stood amongst clustering children in a disheveled line dangerously close to collapse, everyone shifting from one foot to the other awaiting their turn to pick and chose from any number of scrumptious taste-bud tantalizers. This mobile dispenser of lickable luxuries inspired awe in these uninitiated children, as well as the grown men amongst them who had known since childhood the lustfulness an ice cream truck can produce. A few feet ahead of Bernard, Daffyd Lilballerina, the well-dressed owner of the Total Heel shoe shop just down the street a ways, refused to be jostled from his spot in the line, using his rotund frame to throw hip-checks, while his elbows and his bountiful backside nudged away the pack of rowdy kids, all of whom held primal glee in their eyes, hearts and the hullabaloo they hollered.

"Bernard!"

Bernard jumped involuntarily at the husky voice of his Nana James calling from the second story window of her apartment behind him. He'd completely forgotten about her, distracted by deliciousness as he had been. Now he was ensnared. Usually when leaving work at the end of the day he usually avoided dallying on Main Street for inevitably she'd spot him and that would mean having to endure some sort of unpleasant, time-consuming task. He shuddered to think what it might be this time as he reluctantly swiveled around to look up and give a half-hearted acknowledging wave. In doing so, his eyes caught sight of the Kältes, an extremely desiccated old couple who lived in the apartment next to Nana James. They were essentially shut-ins, which is sinisterly unsettling on its own, but what added another level of creepy to an already high amount of eerie, was how they stood in the window clutching the curtains as they leered down with wildly excited faces at the crowd around the ice cream truck. Bernard didn't know them all that well and tried to be more charitable in his estimation of them.

"Perhaps they only want a bit of ice cream," he thought. "That's understandable and not too sinister. However, if they expect me to get it for--"

"Bernard!" Bernard gave another involuntary start. In that brief moment, he'd already forgotten about Nana James. "Come up, I got a chore for ya!" He nodded absentmindedly. Normally robust, she looked as ghostly as the Kälte's. Her head and shoulders were wrapped up in a shawl, too.

"Ah old people," he shrugged, "they're always cold."

"And bring me up a chocolate fudge! Stick's fine, on a sugar cone, if they got it! Better make it a double!"

"Aw fudge and double fudge," cursed Bernard, dropping his head and scuffing his shoe on the sidewalk. Now he wouldn't have enough money to get something for Miss Kennari. "What does the old wildebeest want with me anyhow," her wondered of his Nana James. She was a heaping, hearty strap of leather and beef, hardly the sort who'd need the help of a man only half her size. Although he might like to, he couldn't just ignore the request. He tried that once before and the next time he saw her he found himself in a life-threatening headlock with sharp noogies drilling into his skull.

Finally, it was his turn at the ice cream truck window and he wouldn't be rushed by pernicious nanas or the cajoling kids in line behind him pleading that he "pick any old thing and hurry up!" Any old thing indeed! Any old thing would not do, not with the choices he had before him: flavored ices, fruit juice pops, cream-filled and multi-colored frozen delights.

"God bless that wonderful genius Frank Epperson for inventing the popsicle," he muttered in rhapsodic undertones. "But today is an iced cream day, I do believe."

"Any day's a good day for ice cream," declared the clean-shaven, highly scrubbed young man awaiting his order with a fixed smile. Bernard could only nod in response, so captivated was he by the list of ice cream. There was chocolate, chocolate chip, strawberry, cherry, butter pecan, coffee…an endless ecstasy. Reading the whole list would risk a revolt amongst the pressing plebs at his back, so he settled on his favorite, a single scoop of vanilla in a plain cone. The Fast Freddys of the world could have their sherbets. In his mind, a lick of vanilla was perfection and there was no need to venture beyond it. He would have bought a second, perhaps a strawberry, for Miss Kennari if he'd had money enough after purchasing the double fudge chocolate for his nana, but he knew he'd probably have to forget about the schoolteacher for today, because whatever Nana James had in mind for him would inevitably take forever and a day.

Determined to enjoy his ice cream at least until he got upstairs, Bernard kept his tongue working double-time to catch the drips before they became drops. A thundering rumble of footsteps shook the stairwell as a terror-stricken young man, apparently a delivery boy by the looks of his blue uniform and cap, ran down the stairs, taking them two at a time and barely noticing Bernard as he pushed by.

"Whoa there!" hollered Bernard, holding his sweets out of harm's way. The delivery boy didn't even turn to look, never mind apologize. "Rude," said Bernard and then considered for a moment, "or perhaps I mean odd." The blood had been drained from the boy's face and he flew with abandon as if from some recent fright. At the top of the stairs Bernard saw that Nana James' door was open a crack.

"Hm, now that's most definitely odd," thought Bernard, stopping and craning his neck to peer in. His nose balked at his nana's prevailing and every-present odor. While people of her age often have an "old people smell," something like mothballs mixed with decay, Nana James' was unique, being more akin to the steamroller-strong stench of a football locker room after a particularly grueling game.

As odoriferous as it was, an even more powerful sense distracted Bernard's attention, the feeling of eyes upon the back of his head. When he turned to look, there across the hall in the middle of the Kälte's door opposite his nana's, a pair of eyes stared back at him through the old fashioned peephole. Embarrassment and propriety would dictate their immediate aversion, but not only did they not disappear, they didn't even look away. Neither did Bernard, too fascinating in their revulsion were these eyes that peered lifeless into his own. Finally they vanished. Bernard blinked. Doubting what he'd seen through that overly ornate bronze peephole, he leaned in for a closer look. Two unnaturally huge eyes appeared and ogled him up and down.

A chill ran up his backside, urging him backward into his nana's apartment and into a ghastly scene. Before him, sprawled face down on the floor laid the pallid, motionless body of Nana James. At least one eye he could see remained open and lifeless. Bits of dead leaves clung to her dark gray hair, damp and matted to her head. A trickle of black slime formed at the corner of her ashen lips. Her tongue slipped out and licked up the slime.

"Guess," the voice of Nana James demanded from rigged jaws.

"Oh very well," said Bernard, plopping down on an uncomfortable wooden seat that Nana James had won at an auction just before they demolished some famous baseball stadium Bernard couldn't remember the name of. Both the terrified look of the fleeing delivery boy and those creepy eyes in the peephole had set him on edge, pushing from his mind thoughts of his nana and her pastime of dressing up as and playacting corpses. The initial shocking sight of her put a touch of jelly in his knees and made the painful-to-the-posterior pine planks of the chair almost welcome.

While helping carry a props chest to the backstage area of her high school's theater, Nana James' had been bitten by the acting bug and the ensuing illness landed her in amateur dramatics. However, after stumbling through her lines and over everyone else's, not to mention a few toes, as the beloved spider in *Charlotte's Web* to the unintentional amusement of an audience who were shouting terrible things like "Which one's the spider and which one's the pig?" she was from then on given almost entirely silent roles. It was a fortuitous turn, for a hidden talent was discovered: she was quite adept at playing dead. For her part, she saw it as excellent downtime to rest her muscles or any sports injuries she'd suffered. Since the school's theater director was also its English teacher, Nana James played many a famous fictional character's corpse in the school's productions of adapted classic novels. And so she and the theater program coalesced happily together semester after semester. Over this period she played Addie Bundren in *As I Lay Dying*, the non-skull part of Yorick in *Hamlet*, and a slaughtered cow in *The Jungle*. If only the whale had been dead in *Moby Dick*, she would've fit the role perfectly. Her favorite production was *The Wonderful Wizard of Oz* in which she played the Wicked Witch of the East, for although two thirds of her was stuffed under a cardboard house, when it was over she was allowed to take home the slippers with sparkling rhinestones, since they were so large that only she and full grown men could fit into them. To this day, this very day in fact, Nana James continued reenacting scenes from the books she'd read or read about, always playing the dead characters. Bernard had on occasion walked in on some gruesome scenes, the prom scene from *Carrie* being one of the worst.

"Let's see now. You are," he deliberated while studying the pseudo stiff before him, wishing from the depths of his soul she was wearing more than a straw hat and overalls. The warts sprouting hairs on her wrinkling, liver-spotted back threatened to un-stomach his ice cream.

"Here's a hint," she said, her mouth finally moving noticeably. "Nigger Jim found me like this…though I don't truck with folk that use that word improper and don't wanna hear you using it neither."

Although Bernard wasn't an overly well-read, learned man, there weren't too many fictional characters by that name. Even so, he could not for the life of him remember who the dead character was, nor the name of the book for that matter. The author's name came to him and as he thought on it, Nana James could've been portraying any number of corpses considering how much that Twain brianwig wrote about dead folk.

"Tom something," he pondered. "The Hijinks of Tom and Jerry. No, no. Tom's the other one. It's H something. Harry, Honey, Huckleberry! The Adventures of Huckleberry Hound!"

"Nope and hurry up, I want some of that ice cream 'fore it all runs on to yer hand," she said with an impatience that did little to mask her glee at having a participant in one of her favorite leisure activities.

Bernard thought on, keeping his eyes distractedly moving about the room perusing the posters of sports heroes, a small barrel of carb-loader mix, free weights, and a hemorrhoids donut hanging over the back of his chair, all in an effort to avoid the sight of Nana James' old lady skin. Although he'd done it many a time, he even scrutinized her balls, the rugby balls sitting on her mantle, which she was awarded by the coach after games for her excellent play on the men's varsity team during high school. Spritzerville was without a team, therefore since she was unable to go to games these days she resigned herself to reminiscing about her glory days, all the while remaining absolutely itching to play. Overall it wasn't a large apartment, just a one bedroom with a kitchen-living room combo, but it looked even smaller with Nana James' girth taking up so much of its space. The cramped nature of the place also made it difficult to escape rugby tackles, which Bernard could attest, is not a factor one should overlook in a living arrangement. Bernard, who was not absolutely itching to play rugby, made the mistake of taking a rugby ball off the mantel once. Well, twice actually. Once on purpose and once by accidentally knocking it off. Both times he was sorry. They were keepsakes to Nana James. Their mere presence kept safe some of her fondest memories and when someone handled her balls, it brought out the old rugger in her, firing up an irresistible urge to play. The first time Bernard picked the ball up off the mantel the subsequent and swift flying tackle he received and the crash into the furnishings had given him a concussion, or so he thought. He really couldn't be sure or remember. The second time, a couple days after his thirty-eighth birthday, he was only slightly more prepared and managed to avoid the tackle, but was eventually taken down after an apartment-leveling chase, the whole episode culminating in Bernard giggling and gasping while writhing on the floor with Nana James sitting on his head tickling him mercilessly. "Dignity…dignity," was all he could wheeze out from under her fleshy cheeks.

"Jumping juniper bugs, I'm playing the bloated corpse of Pap Finn from *The Adventures of Huckleberry Finn*!" said Nana James leaping to her feet and wiping the residual slime from the wispy hairs upon her upper lip. It would have been a fine mustache had it been on the face of a fifteen-year-old boy. She snatched the double fudge chocolate ice cream stick from Bernard's sticky chocolate fudge covered hand and bolted it down in one bite, yes, stick and all. "Least I figure he musta been bloated," she said wiping her lips on the back of her hand, "being found dead in a house floatin' on a river. Stands to reason there'd be some seepage through the floorboards in a shoddy old shack built back in them days."

"Yes, no doubt. So was that all or was there something else you asked me up here for, Nana?" inquired Bernard with borderline rude curtness. He wanted to get whatever this chose was over with as soon as possible. It was often time-consuming company-keeping activities that she sought him out for. She never called him up to do physically demanding favors, because even if she'd been the man she wished she'd been born as, instead of the woman she technically was, she would be considered exceptionally spry and muscular, even at her advanced age. She'd never found a man adequate to her needs, so she'd never married. Being a touch too rough and gruff, she had few friends and was terribly lonely, so Bernard found himself acting as an audience for her performances, going through old photos of her playing rugby, plucking the ingrown hairs from the unreachable areas of her body, and other disagreeable tasks. She'd once had him sew up a pair of split slacks, the reason being that she was "no hand at women's work."

"Oh, I don't need anything," she replied this time. In the past, Bernard's knee-jerk reaction would've been to demand, "What in the blazes did you call me up here for then?" However, it is a demonstrated and proven fact that just one pile-driver in reply to such an impertinent question will take the malevolence out of any man. So Bernard prudently waited for her to finish. "It's the Kältes. They want you to--"

"I'd rather not," said Bernard involuntarily as the chills shot up his back again at the thought of the weird eyes staring at him through the Kältes' peephole. Nana James glowered. Bernard cowered.

"They want you to do something or other over there."

"To do what?" asked Bernard lowering his head in submission.

"Search me. I offered to do it for them, but being standoffish and all they said no. Whatever it is, they want a young person like yourself on the job." Bernard wondered at that. He never considered himself young, even when he was young. His status as being forever old was even born out by his mother, who was fond of saying, "You were born an old man."

"Well, I don't know about *young*," he said, glowing in the compliment.

"Alright then Peter Pan, flitter on over there and see what the old grave sniffers want," commanded Nana James as she hustled Bernard out the door before he'd even had time to wash his sticky hands.

The Kälte's white door was freckled brown when he finished knocking on it. He shuddered as the peephole opened and the dead eyes reappeared, disappeared, and went all huge and goggle-eyed again, the irises wandering about like floating saucers. However once they found his own eyes, they wrinkled up and smiled back at him.

Little was known about the enigmatic Kältes. Bernard's curiosity to see how they lived helped him overcome his severe case of the creeps. He'd seen Karol before at a Knit Witties Club meeting but he'd only glimpsed Karl in the window from the street and had never been inside their home.

"Welcome," cooed the highly elderly and utterly gaunt figure of Karol Kälte as she pulled open the door with a straining effort. If it wasn't her big, bouncy, platinum blond wig, the other thing people tended to notice first was her blue skin. People called it blue, but in actuality the skin was translucently white. It was her multitude of oxygen-depleted veins showing through the skin that gave off the bluish tint. One might imagine her abnormally enormous eyes with their long lashes would be noticed first. True, they were large, but they were false, doubly so in that they were also magnified by the thick, black-framed glasses she currently wore. The next eye-catcher was her bright red suit jacket and slacks coupled with matching lipstick upon her gaping wide mouth full of white choppers.

As the door opened wider it revealed a darkened room and a wave of stiflingly warm air rolled out over Bernard. The day was mild and yet it felt hot enough to bake a batch of cookies in there.

"Come in, quickly, quickly. Don't want to let in the cold and catch a chill," Karol said, snapping the door shut just after his rear cleared the frame. He took three steps into the shadowy apartment and tumbled over a box. "Oh, I am ssso sssorry! The delivery boy jussst dropped that off."

"Blasted bugger wouldn't bring it in," shouted the immensely aged Karl Kälte as if he were at the far end of Madison Square Garden and not sitting in his recliner five feet away squinting at Bernard through large, black-rimmed glasses with abnormally tiny eyes. There were allusions to and illusions of ruggedness deep within the old man: broad shoulders that were actually shoulder pads under his khaki shirt, a plain beige garment set off with a pink striped neckerchief; a square jaw hidden because the dimple in his chin stubbornly stuck to its guns on the tip of his jaw while the chin itself had long since gone south. All the rest was plain old decrepitude: the last remnants of white hair still rippling over the crown of his scabby head; bags under his eyes crowded down around his splayed nose, a pink knob mapped by a web of thin, red and blue veins.

"Karl and I can't lift it," said Karol holding up her boney hands as proof of frailty. She frowned down at the object as if chastising it for its heaviness. "Would you be a dear?" Bernard picked himself and the box up. "If you could put it on the sideboard that would be lovely."

Bernard did so while casting glances about the place: faded paintings and family portraits in golden gilded frames, afghan blankets and rugs, furry and fuzzy throw pillows, lamps with velvety shades and long tassels. That was enough for him. He made for the door with great hopes of a quick escape, saying, "Well if that's all, I'll be off!"

"Oh no! No, no, no. We didn't asssk you over for that," Karol clarified. Bernard thought she said "ass" and had to disguise his chortle as a cough.

"What is it you'd like me to do then?" he was finally able to ask.

"Have a ssseat dearie," said Karol, laying her hand upon his arm. Her skeletal fingers felt like icicles searing a fierce frigidity into his skin that quite shocked Bernard.

"What in the name," he shouted, yanking his arm away and staring unbelieving down at her liver-spotted, fragile hand, so pale and full of death. If she had something catchy, he didn't want it.

Karol and Karl Kälte
Definitely not Carol Channing and Charles Nelson Reilly

"Oh, you are ssso *warm*." She drove such emphasis into the last word that one would think her life depended upon it. He couldn't understand how she could be so cold considering the stifling heat in the apartment. Attempting to brush aside the incident so as not to insult them, he complimented them on the décor and turned to sit, but all the seats, aside from Karl's, had plastic covering them and he hesitated to sit on anything so like preserved artifacts. However, he had been invited to have a seat, so he picked the rocking chair.

"Not that one," hollered Karl, "It's two hundred years old and worth more than your life!"

"Oh, yesss," said Karol, a hand to her mouth and her face drawn down in apology. "The love ssseat isss more comfortable, dear." Bernard shrugged and moved to the love seat. "Would you like a beverage? Tea? I'll make usss tea!" She began shuffling out of the room and teetered to a stop before rounding the corner. "Would you be a dear and lend a hand?" Bernard followed her into the kitchen where the kettle was already bubbling away on the verge of whistling. Heavy, slow steam rose above it into the warm air. With the cups on the tray, loose-leaf tea placed in a strainer within a teapot, and the sugar at the ready, Karol appeared to have everything in hand.

"Milk with your tea?" she asked while slipping a hand-sized brass container from the back of a cupboard and pouring its contents into one of the cups. Bernard noticed it was a flask. "Oh!" She looked as if she'd been caught by a chef adding something to his soup. "Karl likesss a little ssspiccce in hisss tea," she explained, tucking away the bottle.

"Shall I grab the milk?" asked Bernard reaching out for the refrigerator handle.

"No," she blurted, recoiling and looking a ghast. She held up her hands as if to ward off a ghost, looking genuinely disturbed by the very idea of the refrigerator.

"Anything the matter?" he asked, his forward momentum moving his hand ever closer to the door handle.

"Don't! Don't touch it. We don't like the young onesss messsing about with the appliancccesss." The flash of mania subsided and eventually relented to her wide-mouthed, toothy smile. "And we don't want fingerprintsss on the door, now do we? We'll clean you up in a jiffy!" She grabbed his sticky hands and led him to the sink. Again, her cold hands stung his skin, but this time he was better prepared and remembered his manners, rcfraining from pulling away, allowing her frozen skin to sear into his. After all, he surmised, aren't all old people always cold like this?

128

"Oh, your handsss are ssso warm." Her eyes closed and all of the lines in her face lifted so that she became the very picture of enchantment, a picture with an antique frame, but nonetheless. She held his hands under the warm tap water to wash them, which did little to alleviate the icy chill of her own. Patting them dry, she wrapped his hands in a tea towel and held them bundled up tight to her bosom. Bernard's relief was immense when she finally stopped touching him. There was something perverse in the way she caressed his hands, rubbing them sensually with the towel and delighting in their warmth.

"Stop messing about in there and bring me my tea," bellowed Karl. Karol abruptly dropped Bernard's hands and put on a heavy pair of oven mitts before taking a small pitcher of milk from the refrigerator. She placed it on a tray as part of a bronze service set.

In the living room, Bernard settled into the loveseat. Karol poured out the tea, while Karl rested his eyes. He wasn't sleeping. He made that clear when Karol nudged him and placed his cup on the well-doilied end-table at his elbow. He cleared his throat, grumbled and gave Bernard the evil-eye over a surly sneer.

"Your auntie or grandmother or whatever that is over there," he said pointing at the door to indicate Nana James, "she said you were a good boy that liked to do a good deed now and then for us old 'uns." Though starting to feel a bit weary, Bernard's hopes lifted at the thought that they might finally be getting to the actual reason for his visit. But then Karl paused and looked vaguely about the room, his gaze finally falling upon the window. "Saw you playing with the kiddos down there on the street," he said.

"There'sss nothing quite like the young to reinvigorate one'sss ssself," injected Karol with no small amount of passion.

"One's elf? You own an elf?" This really lifted Bernard's spirits. He glanced anew about the room.

"No, one'sss *ssself*," she corrected.

"Oh, I see," he said, but he didn't see and still thought they might have an elf stashed somewhere. Elves are rare and interesting creatures, and aside from a few bad apples, Bernard had no strong objection to this form of faery. In his opinion, they were people, too, and if the Kältes were harboring one in their apartment, trying to get it reinvigorated, then why not throw a few of the booger-machines at it if that's what made it happy? In fact, if a sacrificial babe was needed, he knew of a certain wigmonger who had a rather disagreeable child that Bernard didn't think would be much missed. Certainly they'd give the kid back to its parents when the elf

129

was done with it. What would an elf do with a child? He had no clue, these interesting ideas not being the sort of thing a haberdasher normally concerned himself with.

"Benjamin, is it?" asked Karl as his backside wrestled with the cushions under it.

"Bernard, actually."

"Benedict, you ever do a hard day's gardening in your life?" Bernard was put off-guard and had no immediate answer for a question that had in all likelihood never been asked of anyone anywhere ever. "I didn't think so, not a softy like you," said Karl, giving him an up-down dismissive going over.

"Do you still garden?" asked Bernard.

"Do I still garden? Hell and damnation boy, I hardly can get out of this chair! But I did, and a lot of it too! Cripesake, up until a couple years ago, I was hoeing rows and sowing seeds since you were suckling your mama's soft serve."

"Oh dear, really!" protested a disgusted Karol, flapping butterfly hands at him. Karl waved dismissively back at her and plunged into a lengthy lecture on azaleas with no foreseeable end in sight. On a purely hobbyist's level, Bernard had puttered about in his backyard a bit, never quite accomplishing what he set out to do. Nonetheless, he'd done enough of it to know that it was not the ultra-manly endeavor Mr. Kälte was making it out to be. The almost entirely one-sided conversation rambled on and within a few minutes Bernard was no longer paying sufficient attention to know just why the old man, sitting there chair-bound like a lazy Buddha except for the crossed legs, was lifting and flexing his flabby arm. If it was meant to show how strong gardening had made him, Bernard highly doubted the boast. Sure, underneath the flab, the wrinkles, the peculiar pelvic bulge under the high-riding belt that was not quite stomach and not quite groin, somewhere in there could lay dormant a raging bull of a man. While considering all this, Bernard leaned farther back into the loveseat. Plastic or not, he found it incredibly comfortable, almost too comfortable. With the oppressive heat of the room and Karl's endless nattering, Bernard was on the verge of resting his eyes.

"Benny, dear." Karol's trembling, high treble voice in his ear shot Bernard awake. "While Karl's taking a break from his story," a quick glance showed that Karl slumbered again, "perhapsss you'd like to admire hisss trophy collection upon the mantle." The feeble old woman stretched out a helping hand, but Bernard declined it and with an effort excavated himself out of the depths of the cushy loveseat. He skirted the far side of the coffee table, eluding Karol's reaching fingers and wobbled stiff-legged over to the fireplace to scan the many gardening awards: ribbons, plaques, and various other trophies Karl won back in the day. One particular large pewter cup embossed with "1ˢᵗ Place for Wattle Work" was full to the brim with gold coins. Cluttered together among the trophies stood a number of unused candlesticks in ornate, copper holders.

"I suppose I should really be going," said Bernard, turning around and finding Karol sitting on the loveseat nestling herself into the spot he'd just vacated, luxuriating in the cozy warmth of his remaining body heat. She appeared to be in a semi-catatonic bliss, what with her eyes closed and a contented grin on her face. Bernard thought it a little strange, but when she let out a kitten's purr he became officially unnerved and was more than ready to leave.

"T.V.!" piped up Karl straight out of his slumber, startling Bernard. "Bertie, see if you can't fiddle with the rabbit ears and get something in. I don't know technology like you young folk. Go on and give it a shot."

"I'm perhaps not as young as you think," said Bernard, and as he told them his real age the Kältes visibly deflated. Bernard didn't notice. He was pleased with being thought young and had already gladly wedged his way in behind the ancient television set, playing around with the metal antennas with their tinfoil flags waving about. His Grandma Ellie had a television, but she didn't let him touch it. Only a particular nephew of hers was allowed near it. So Bernard relished this foray into the world of technology, even if it only amounted to futile attempts to get reception on the Kälte's set. "It feels like the future," he happily mused to himself. An unusual thought for a man so happily mired in the past. He didn't have the money to purchase a television or even half the things the Kältes owned. They had beautiful, if old, furnishings. Who else had real crystal chandeliers in every room, even the kitchen? They probably even had one in the bathroom. "May I use your bath--"

"Ho! Ho! You had something there. Go back! Do what you did before," hollered Karl.

"There?" asked Bernard, holding the antennas about where he thought they'd been at the moment Karl saw his something.

"I don't know," said Karl, squinting, grimacing and contorting his face in all ways in order to improve his sight. "Can't see half of nothing with these old things." Taking the glasses he wore by one of the temples between his thumb and forefinger, he wiggled the thick-lensed, chunky black spectacles rapidly up and down. "Blind without 'em and now seems

I'm just about as bad off with 'em." He went on complaining about his poor eyesight, forgetting all about the television, until eventually his diatribe died down and he slipped into a light snooze. Bernard was relieved to finally be able to put his arms down and get out from behind the television, an area not unlike a dusty sauna.

"Sssweetsss," slithered Karol's slippery voice into his ear making him jump. She was right behind him holding out an intricately hand-designed porcelain bowl filled with ribbon candy. "We know how you love the sssweetsss, you children."

"Children?" shouted a fully alert Karl, shooting half out of his chair.

"No, dear. False alarm. Go back to sleep."

"I'm not sleeping, just resting my--" began Karl, falling back asleep before he finished.

"We love," began Karol, stressing the word love as if it truly meant the world to her, "chil...the young onesss. We sssaw you playing out in the ssstreet with your little friendsss. Do you think any of them would like to come up and enjoy sssome candy?" As she asked with a desperately imploring look, she held the bowl up to Bernard again. He grabbed a piece and with it came the whole clump of candy, stuck together into one giant mass. Before snapping off a piece and putting the rest back, he saw that underneath the candy sitting in the bottom of the bowl were handfuls of gold coins. It formed the opinion within him that these Kältes had so much money that they were running out of places to put it.

Bernard tried to explain that those children on the street weren't what he would call "friends," so much as annoyances getting in the way of him and his ice cream, but she wouldn't hear it, so certain was she of his connection to the youth of Spritzerville.

"I'll bet it'sss lovely being around them all. It warmsss the heart." The pleasure left her face, which scrunched up into a wince. She took off her glasses, laying them on the coffee table at her end of the couch and rubbed her eyes. "Oh thessse glasssesss. They were fine up until a few daysss ago and now their giving me the Dickensss." While Karl slept, Karol held the floor as "speaker of the house." Youth was clearly her favorite topic, Bernard noted, and now he was beginning to understand just how much it meant to her. She clung to her own youth desperately with glossy lipstick, the powder layered on to her face and that pristine wig. As her monologue went on, he spotted lotion bottles poking out from behind picture frames and lamps. Bernard had plenty of time to ponder this as the one-way conversation had devolved into an expansive grocery list of her

132

old-age bodily grievances. In fact, time had never seemed so eternal to Bernard then as he endured the endless monotony of old person complaints: rheumatism, arthritis, osteoporosis, high blood pressure, cataracts, macular degeneration, shingles, an undiagnosed rash, unreliable bowels and other things no one wants to hear about. Every tick of their two grandfather clocks seemed like the passing of days. His head, heavy with the want of sleep, nodded left and right, forwards and back, each time he caught himself before falling asleep, until the last roll forward shot him out of the loveseat and onto his feet, where he stood straight up, astonished and awake. The sudden movement finally startled Karol speechless.

"I ah, well, I suppose…" Bernard tottered over his words and feet as he pitched towards the door.

"Hello! What?" shouted Karl clear out of a sound sleep. "Leaving us so soon?"

After mumbling a few yawning words about how he "must…must go," Bernard turned to wave and there was Karol right behind him looking terribly blue and quivering with cold. She grasped at his hand and the tips of her fingers dug into his flesh like icepicks.

"Ssstay, ssstay," she pled in whining hisses, her un-bespectacled, desirous eyes lustily running up and down his body, though quite close up since she couldn't see very well, which lessened the passion a tad. Bernard's unease did not lessen.

"No, no really, I must go," he said. "I feel a touch poorly." The seemingly insignificant 'touch' turned into grand theft as his wealth of health drained from him as fast as a bank liquidation during a catastrophic financial meltdown. An uncontrollable shiver shuddered through him and soon he was fatigued and aching all over, as if he were being steamrolled by a burly cold or flu with a license to operate heavy machinery. "I'm sorry, I don't know what's come over me. I think I'm coming down with something." As he spoke he looked at Karol and, although his eyes were going a tad fuzzy, it was plain that she'd regained some of her vitality. She looked much healthier, younger even. Her once blue, wrinkled skin turned pink and smooth. She stood confidently erect, her breasts no longer dangling to her beltline, her hair shimmering in the light and a twinkle livened in her eye…a devious twinkle.

"That'sss too bad," she said. The strong and un-quavering words lacked compassion. With renewed strength, her hands clamped vice-like upon his arm and her voice took on a vehement tone. "You will come back again when you are well. You will bring along sssome of your young friendsss."

"Yesss, bring more of the young onesss next time," said Karl reaching out from his seat towards Bernard with a yellowy nailed hand grown claw-like, bent and gnarled from arthritis. In his foggy-headed state, Bernard swore Karl had started that hissing lisp, just like Karol.

"Yeah...I--I will," said Bernard, but the words were hardly his own. They were distant and felt drawn from him rather than spoken by him.

"Promissse," commanded Karol, wrapping her arms around him, drawing him in and nearly hugging the life out of him. After Bernard promised that he would "bring back more young onesss," only then did Karol release him.

His clammy palms slipped along the railing as he stepped gingerly on unsteady legs down the stairs that were blurring and rocking side to side. Like a subdued echo from deep within some vague, distant valley, Nana James called after him as he stumbled from the building.

"Bernard? Bernard?"

He staggered home, heeding nothing and nearly getting lost in the oncoming dark and confusion of his mind.

"The flu. Most definitely the flu," he slurred as he fell upon his bed and blacked out.

The blaring rays of the morning sun rogered his eyes open. Apparently, there was a bear in his bedroom.

"Perhaps it's a walrus," he debated silently with himself, squinting over an extra and very warm, knit blanket as the hulking beast trundled about the room. When it lurched towards the bed, Bernard closed his eyes and pretended to sleep. "Play possum like raccoons do and maybe it'll leave us alone. Or maybe we are sleeping, what?" He couldn't tell. The dreamy vision provided proof a'plenty of his asleepedness, but in his delirious condition he couldn't be sure of anything.

An orangey afternoon sun played upon his pajama sleeve. Someone or something's hand lay upon his forehead.

"He's burning up," said a soul all too worried, thought Bernard. His eyes closed, for how long he wasn't sure. When he opened them again he imagined the thing on the chair beside the bed to be an elf. The vision cleared and came together, revealing a little girl engrossed in a picture book.

"Jenny?" Bernard managed to slur out.

"Momma's in the kitchen," the little girl uttered. Bernard doubted very much that his mother was in the kitchen. Then it dawned on him the girl meant her own mother. This was his niece's five-year-old daughter swinging her legs and never looking up from her book. It might have been a book of spells, he considered, and this creature just as likely a pixie, one of those devilish tricksters playing him for a fool. He wanted to get up to squish the pixie under his shoe while simultaneously showing his niece's young daughter that he was okay, there was no need to worry. But it took all his strength just to crack open one blurry eye. The little girl was being led by the hand from the room. She turned and waved at him. He tried to smile and wave back. He was so concerned that she might worry herself to ruin over his health, then realized she would be fine, she was a little girl.

"What does she care," he raged inwardly in an unprovoked fury. "She's not sick! I'm the sick one, I'm the one that's going to die. No one else cares." He clenched his teeth and balled up his fists. "I'm dying and no one cares!" He shook until the shakes overtook him and he sweat all over, then passed out. A cool washcloth slid down over his eyes and it dawned on him that someone had been there to take care of him. He had not been left completely alone. Realizing this calmed him some. But then the concern that he would be left alone would rise again and his mind would race in these never ending circles like some infinite Ouroboros of useless cyclical grief and relief. Within minutes he was tossing about in bed, throwing off the blankets. Shivers and sweats alternated in waves until, weakened by the exertions, he dropped into an all-embracing sleep that threatened never to release him.

Beyond his will and notice, his world changed. Blankets were replaced. Cool, damp clothes covered his forehead. The room dimmed. The room lightened. Blankets were reduced. Cool, damp cloths covered his forehead. On and on it went.

"Who are these troublesome beings? Leave me be!" he shouted a few days later as he thrashed about the bed, kicking off the covers, only to begin shaking with cold immediately after.

"Calm down, Uncle Beanie," said a soothing voice above him. His heart lifted and he slipped back into the darkness.

Always there was someone there to replace the blankets, to keep him warm or to keep him cool. Always there was someone trying to feed him that awful peas porridge in a pot nine days old and cleaning it off the floor when he threw it up. In his more lucid moments, he was annoyed by the attention one moment and then thankful beyond words for it the next. He didn't understand what was going on until days into this prolonged illness when he finally learned to let it go and relax enough to quell the mad, spinning wheels of his mind. Once he became aware of the world around him again, on a morning in which he awoke to the tinny, static-laden sounds of a be-bopping tune coming from a transistor radio, he remembered his store and realized he hadn't been attending to it all this time. Frantically he struggled out of bed, but a hand upon his chest eased him back into the pillow. His old school chum, Knobby, got up from a chair by the bed, placed the toady, Gaiety, by Bernard's side and told him to relax. Bernard didn't want to relax and would've made another break for it, but he didn't want to upset his pet. He stroked its back once, twice, thrice and then fell back to sleep.

Like detonating TNT, Bernard exploded awake with a blindingly brilliant idea burning away in his brain. His arms and legs thrashed about with the infuriating covers as he scrambled to get out of bed.

"Nana James," he shouted.

"Settle down, dear. It's your Grandma Ellie. Your nana left an hour ago. But if you don't lie back down, I'll go get her and she'll make you lie back down." Bernard lied back down, though the reproach did nothing to staunch his enthusiasm.

"Grandma Ellie, I've just come up with the most wondrous way to save Miss Kennari's position at the school!"

"I didn't know it needed saving or that you took such an interest," said Grandma Ellie, casting a questioning eye upon him.

"Ah yes, well, it's nothing. Hate to see the local school closed down is all. Just doing my civic duty, you know, as a community leader in the business…community." If Bernard's speech were a dance it would be called "The Meander." His words were sauntering about with two left feet and he knew it. Embarrassment crept into his conscience and he would've done a swan dive into a deep coma if he could've managed it, but he was feeling too well.

"That's very community spirited of you, dear," said Grandma Ellie pushing the uncomfortable conversation along. "What's your plan?"

"Thank you. Well, you know the Kältes?"

"Those old coots on Main Street?"

"It's pronounced Kälte, but yes. They're loaded, you see, and they love kids…actually, I don't know that they even like kids. I think it might have something to do with an elf they own that needs reinvigorating. Apparently kids do the trick. Don't look at me like that, that's what they said. Anyhow, if I can talk them into sponsoring the local education of at least one student it'll save Miss--the schoolteacher's job!"

"Miss The Schoolteacher will be very pleased, I'm sure," said Grandma Ellie, who saw no fault in the plan and in fact she thought it a noble idea. Not that he needed any encouragement, but what little she gave him was enough to vault him out of bed. There was work to be done and he was going to do it! "You get right back in bed, young man!" demanded Grandma Ellie. She was not an imposing person in stature to say the least, but what she lacked in brawn she more than made up for in bossiness when she held the moral high ground. "Come along, you're still not well. Back to bed with you!" He realized she was right. Standing there, dizziness whirled the room around and his legs shook with the effort. In Bernard's strength-sapped state, Grandma Ellie had no problem pushing him back into bed.

"Eat some of this. Go on, eat!" She said minutes later upon returning to the bedroom with a bowl of peas porridge and forcing a spoonful down his gullet. "You've gone all pale again. I hope the flu's not coming back. I told you not to exert yourself."

"No, I feel fine," he said after swallowing hard. "I just really hate…peas por--" An involuntary volley of mushy peas shot from his mouth.

"You only had to say so, dear," said Grandma Ellie wiping at her face and calling from the bathroom, "You remind me of that poor, unfortunate girl…what's her name?"

"Anne Frank?"

"No, no. The girl, the uncontrollable one, thrashing about all crazy like."

"Helen Keller?" Bernard couldn't think right now. On top of his own Kennari concerns, he feared he'd offended his grandmother.

"Linda Blair," she hollered triumphantly and came back into the room a moment later wearing a chipper smile and carrying a plate loaded with pig bits "Very well then, Mister Pickypants, how would you like bacon instead? Your little friend left behind a few rashers." She laid the plate by his side.

"Oh yes, please!" Bernard's appetite came back with a resounding rumble from his belly, now slightly less rounded than usual. As he ate, Grandma Ellie briefed him on the latest news. Upon learning how many family and friends had rallied around to look after him, taking turns nursing him or looking after his store - Knobby had turned quite a tidy profit in the interim - a warm glow of thankfulness spread over Bernard. He was happy to not only have his health, but to know that more people cared about him than he'd ever imagined.

He propped his pillow against the headboard, took up pen, paper and a hardcover book to write on, then dashed off a few thank you notes. He then got down to the serious business of composing a letter to the Kältes that detailed his plan, while indicating the pressing need for a prompt reply. He hoped for more success than his failed plan involving the Poop Baby. In fact, he pinned his last hope to this letter.

"There's really only one week within which to put this new plan into action," he said finishing the letter after Grandma Ellie left and Nana James arrived. He handed it to her and she brought it to the Kältes, returning the very next day with their reply letter. Bernard broke the wax seal and tore it open. His eyes sprinted across the words.

"They've agreed! With a stipulation, but they've agreed none the less!"

"What's the problem?" asked Nana James as she lifted his naked body into the tub. This was unnecessary protested Bernard, but she wouldn't listen.

"Something about how I've got to bring any prospective young ones...they mean students...any students by their place, so they can *feel their worth*. I think they mean so that they can *get a feel for* their worth. They probably want to make sure they're backing the right horse. Seems fair to me." Bernard clapped his hands and rubbed them vigorously together. "Oh hurray!"

Normally Bernard would've been more impatient to get back to work. However, for the first time in a long time, something else took precedence over the haberdashery. He dare not say it aloud, but he believed it might be love. Yes, he loved Miss Kennari! He loved her so much he was willing to go against his better judgment and sacrifice the betterment of his business in order to do this thing for her, with the added benefit of furthering his own desire in obtaining more time with which to woo her.

Essentially confined to bed, he used this down time to rush through a litany of letters and send out a plethora of parrot posts all in an effort to put his plan in motion. He contacted any Spritzervillian with a boy or girl in grammar school and did his darnedest to cajole them into bringing their child back to Spritzerville's one-room schoolhouse. Few replied. All rejected the idea. It seemed things had changed since he was a boy and his parents had dropped him off at the nearest boarding school the first chance they got. Parents nowadays, he discovered, wanted the best for their children. A free elementary school education, paid for by the Kältes, was not enticing enough. Parents were thinking long-term educational goals. Once he figured this out Bernard revised his strategy and came up with a new scheme. He made a promise that a child graduating from the Spritzerville school was guaranteed placement in an ivy school. The new scheme absolutely thrilled the Beardsleys, who took him up on the offer immediately, no questions asked. That they asked no questions was a great relief to Bernard, because he might have had to reveal that the "ivy" school was not an Ivy League university, just a junior high school in the nearby town of Wilson that had a dangerously prodigious amount of poison ivy growing about its grounds. Students were constantly sent home with horrendous rashes. Many parents were removing their children from the school, so the administrators were desperate to attract new ones. Bernard had to admit it was underhanded, but...

"Anyone who thinks a child graduating from a podunk elementary school merits automatic admission into one of the most prestigious universities in the world, deserves what's coming to him."

The Beardsley boy was all he needed, just one student to keep the Spritzerville school open and Miss Kennari in town. Once no longer ill, Bernard collected the child from his parents, who were willing, eager even, to leave their son in the hands of essentially a stranger who'd fed them a dream. It made Bernard think that perhaps they weren't as concerned for their child's wellbeing as they should be, after all, they'd named their boy Sioux.

Bernard dragged the slow, shy Sioux to the Kältes. Karol opened the door, let out a shrill squeal, grabbed the boy and slammed the door in Bernard's face.

"Well, that's a fine how do you do!" He was surprised. He was miffed. He was massaging a sharp pain on his arm where Karol had gripped it in order to wrench Sioux away from him. Up until then he'd forgotten all about the day on which he'd become ill, but like a sluggish, somewhat dimwitted bolt of lightning, he was struck by the recollection of his flu-like ordeal and how it all started the moment Karol had grabbed him in that manner during his last visit.

"She made me sick?" he wondered confused at first, but then he recalled the helpless sensation of his strength being sapped, his very life's essence being sucked from him. "Yes, right through the very fingertips of that...that old...biddy! That frigid, old bag is going to steal the warmth right out of the boy unfortunately named Sioux!" A moral twinge tugged at his scruples. "Damn scruples acting up again." He scratched at his groin and grimaced, but this twinge was all metaphor. Screwing up his courage and determination with the conviction that he alone was the catalyst, nay, the very cause of this calamity and must be the remedy, he stepped back and leapt at the door shoulder first, pulling up just short to consider whether it be advisable for a man of his age and medical history (that devastating melon balling accident of a few years past couldn't be ignored) to undergo such strenuous activity. "There's no time for a doctor's visit!" he declared lunging at the door, remembering it was made of thick oak, skidding to a halt and knocking.

"Yesss?" asked a perturbed Karol as she whipped open the door with more annoyance than she'd ever shown him before. Bernard hadn't planned what to say, but then it hit him, more specifically it hit his nose.

"Why, is that tapioca pudding I smell," he inquired, sticking a foot in the doorway.

"Yesss, I'm making some now," she said, moving to block Bernard from entering the apartment any farther. "Ssso, how can we help you, Mr. Wimple?"

"Ah. Well. I thought I smelled pudding." This tête-à-tête was not holding Karol's interest and she inched the door closed against the pressure of Bernard's obstinate toe, clearly was not planning on inviting him in. "And, uh, I wondered if I might prevail upon you, knowing how delicious your pudding no doubt must be, to, you know, perhaps try some?" Karol's face went all queer, stuck as it was between the offensive feeling of being put out and the pleasurable sensation of receiving a compliment. She backed down and the door eased open enough for Bernard to stick his head in.

"Give him his pudding and get him on his way," grumbled Karl, who's chair was now sitting right up close to the boy, Sioux, seated timidly in the loveseat looking more than a little frightened of these strangers.

"I have to get the little guy out of there," thought Bernard, "but how?" The moment he attempted it assuredly the Kältes would get their icy hands on the both of them and that would be the end. He had to think of something. He needed more time. Karl's creepy claw crawled along his knee and on to the couch, inching ever closer to the boy. Bernard racked his brain and something small rattled free.

"Before the pudding, I had some gardening questions I wanted to put to you, Karl."

"Ey, what's that? Gardening you say?" Karl's claw retracted as he turned towards Bernard. "Ask! Ask now and be gone!"

"Oh, I…um, let's see." Bernard strolled about the room in no particular rush pretending to admire the trophies and furnishings, deliberately dragging out the pauses between each word. "Well, first can we turn up the heat? I feel a bit of a chill." Karol flipped the thermostat up and stood by with her arms folded. Her skin was back to its wrinkled and blue norm.

"I'll go get the pudding," she spat. "We can eat it while you talk and kill two birdsss."

Bernard waited a moment for her to finish before putting in, "With one stone, you mean?" She paused before answering with a sly "sssure" and then stalked off to the kitchen.

"Uh! How about a fire, in the fireplace? And here, Karl, wouldn't you be more comfortable by the fire?" Without waiting for an answer, Bernard grabbed the back of Karl's chair with him in it and swung it across the floor, scrunching up an area rung, knocking over the wire-mesh magazine rack, but otherwise landing the chair and Karl safely by the fireplace, well away from the boy.

"What the blazes?" hollered Karl.

"There, that's much better!" Bernard fixed the mess he'd made, then swiped his palms together and smiled at his handy work. Karl didn't look very pleased, but while Bernard labored to start a fire, he prodded him for his questions and finding them lacking, plowed into a general history of gardening. The subject tired both lecturer and listeners. As he wound up his oratory on the historical rise and fall of the tulip in the Netherlands and segued into a rant against today's modern cloches without a care in the world for continuity, Bernard nearly nodded off and would've done a face-plant into the fire he'd just started if it he weren't shocked awake by Karol's shrill voice.

"Come child, help Auntie in the kitchen," she said in cloying tones, slinking back into the room and slithering up alongside the boy, coaxing him with long white fingers that groped at his clothes and hair. The scraping of her nails along the skin of his cherubim chin triggered the shakes in the boy.

"No!" cried Bernard so loud it surprised everyone, even himself. He scrambled across the room, jumped over the coffee table and sat down beside the boy, putting an arm around him. "Ah, no, that is. A growing boy needs to learn about gardening."

"Hear, hear!" agreed Karl, which stymied Karol's attempt much to Bernard's relief. Under his tight grasp, the boy's shaking subsided somewhat. Karol leered, hissed and reluctantly withdrew to the kitchen.

"The boy'd rather sit here on his Uncle Karl's knee and listen to his stories anyhow, wouldn't ya boy?" The boy's shook like a can in a paint can shaker. "Ah boys," said Karl, but what he meant by it Bernard couldn't be sure. He was just glad when the old man dropped it and began

141

speechifying upon the best soil composition for drupes. It didn't take long before the warmth of the room and boring topic had everyone's eyelids growing heavy.

"Fight it, fight it," whispered Bernard into the boy's ear. A clattering came from the kitchen.

"I could ussse the asssissstanccce of a young man, preferably a boy," called Karol. Bernard held on tighter to Sioux. To his relief, Karl waved away her request as if it were a pesky mosquito and went on talking. Eventually Karol brought in a tub of tapioca pudding. She dropped it on the coffee table in front of the loveseat, shot a menacing glare at Bernard before heading back into the kitchen. Bernard watched her go and then turned as inconspicuously towards the boy as he could.

"Don't let them hug up on you boy or it's the end," he whispered into Sioux's ear. He meant only to warn the boy, but he might as well have told him a bedtime horror story. Never had he seen a child look more thoroughly terrified. It crushed Bernard's heart to think he'd put a child in harm's way. He would get him out of there or die trying! "Perhaps now's the chance," he thought. With Karol in the kitchen, they'd just have to get by Karl. As Bernard glanced up his heart leapt to see that Karl was falling asleep. His plan to stoke the fire and warm up the room to a nice sleeping temperature worked. The old man's lips were still moving as he grumbled something about radicles, but his eyelids - just about shut - fluttered open at the ting-ting clink of glass bowls coming from the kitchen. Karol would be back at any moment. If Bernard was going to act, it would have to be within the next few seconds. If he grabbed the kid, made a break for it and Karl woke up, with his chair so very close to the door, there was no way he wouldn't catch them. "Unless," thought Bernard, "unless he couldn't see well enough to know what was going on." A few agonizing seconds ticked off the grandfather clocks. Karl's eyelids clamped shut. Bernard dove across the room, carefully slid off the coke bottle thick-lensed glasses off the old man's face and plunged them deep into the pudding. A second later Karol slid back into the room carrying bowls and spoons. From her perspective, it appeared a bright-eyed Bernard was just finishing up a bounce on the sofa and licking a dab of pudding from his finger.

"Naughty boy, wait your turn. And don't bounccce on the furnissshingsss," she said. She doled out portions for everyone, slopping down a miserly spoonful for Bernard. Each time she dipped the spoon into the tapioca tub he held his breath, hoping she wouldn't scoop up Karl's glasses. He grabbed a bowl, laid it ever so carefully upon Karl's lap hoping not to wake him and then remained standing right where he was in the middle of the room, blocking Karol's view of her husband, hoping she wouldn't notice he was missing his glasses. She couldn't have cared less. All her attention was on the boy. She longingly admired him slopping up his pudding and wiping his profusely running nose on his sleeve. But then she winced and took off the glasses she was wearing to rub her eyes.

"Are your eyes bothering you? Maybe there's something wrong with your glasses." Without asking he grabbed them from her, inadvertently brushing against her chest.

"Oh! Mister Wimple!" she cried in astonishment.

"Let me take a look at them in the light by the window." He pretended to inspect the specs, but it was the window he was actually checking out. As he feared, it was locked. His fear turned to horror at what Karol said next.

"Child, give Auntie Karol a big hug and kisss…"

Bernard yanked closed the long, satiny drapes, throwing the apartment into darkness all but for the wavering orange light of the fire that cast gyrating shadows about the room.

"Oh that'sss too dark. I can't sssee," hissed Karol. Spinning around, Bernard flung the glasses into the fire. Under cover of the shadowy light he grabbed the boy, tucking him under his arm like a football and leapt over the coffee table, swerved wide around Karl's chair on his way to the door, but doubled back when Karl growled awake, flailing his claws about in the darkness.

"What's going on? I can barely see!"

"The young onesss are essscaping!" wailed Karol, desperately kicking her legs and scratching at the air while extracting herself from the depths of the loveseat. Karl spotted Bernard making for the door and roared, upsetting his pudding as he lashed out. The old man's momentum sent him tumbling forward from his chair on to the floor. Bernard jumped over him with Karol coming up from behind, hissing and snarling as she clawed at the shadows. Bernard threw open the door and was pulling it closed behind him when Karol's bony hand clamped on to his arm. Immediately his strength drained away and he dropped the boy. With his free hand he grasped the doorknob and fell with all his weight backwards out into the hallway, yanking the door shut and crushing not only his own arm, but crunching Karol's brittle hand too. He rolled across the hall, found his feet, and he and the boy tumbled down the steps with the howling banshee shrieks of Karol Kälte echoing in the stairwell.

By the time he had Sioux safely back home, Bernard had broken into a cold sweat and gone all foggy-headed. His nerves were still up, which made him shake uncontrollably while his eyes flew about wildly manic. After blurting out the bizarre, albeit truthful story of what had transpired to Sioux's horrified parents, they ushered their boy inside and slammed the door in Bernard's face.

From there he went straight home and straight to bed. A horrible sleepless night of sweats and chills crept along until he passed out at dawn. But he sprung awake just before noon feeling good enough to go to work, he decided. For half the workday he stood behind the counter of his haberdashery sneezing and blowing his nose, but always keeping a big, artificially chipper smile on his face for the many well-wishers that popped their heads in the door. Some of them even bought a few items. It made him feel pretty good all things considered, at least right up until the late afternoon when the very air about him went all wonky, the floor turned a tad wavy and he collapsed behind the counter. He awoke feeling much better two hours later, just before closing time.

Going home and climbing under the covers would've been the smart move. All the same, he couldn't resist swinging by the school in hopes of seeing Miss Kennari. As always seems to happen when one's in a rush, one thing or another stands in the way. While locking up his shop, Myles Thyghmaster the zombie turkey living in the apartment above, showed up with his monthly rent check.

"The rent's not due 'til next week, Mr. Thyghmaster. Good day!" Bernard donned his bowler and, swiveling on his heel, headed off down the sidewalk.

"I'm deeply troubled for the necessity of disagreeing with you, Mr. Wimple sir," said Thyghmaster catching him up, "but it is the last of the month. Of this I'm quite sure."

A very polite, though perturbing to Bernard's way of thinking, argument ensued in which Bernard finally had to admit defeat as it dawned on him that he'd lost a whole week being sick.

Leaving a bewildered Thyghmaster in the lurch, Bernard hot-footed it to the school, where he found Superintendent Nes locking a chain to the front doors.

"The school is closed until further notice," replied the superintendent to Bernard's babbled questioning.

"But what about Miss Kennari?" he managed to get out.

"Kennari left town. Found another job in, where was it? March Fjord? Yes, March Fjord."

Bernard couldn't remember walking home, but he must have, because hours later he was sitting at his own kitchen table with his pet toady, stroking its back and feeding it its favorite, brown sugar water. "It wasn't meant to be. It was never meant to be." Bernard kept a stiff upper lip, while Gaiety wept for him. "It will be all right, my friend. It will have to be or what else is there?"

The next day, Bernard went to the authorities. The Warden of the Weirdlings removed the Kältes from Spritzerville after prolonged legal proceedings in which the old, almost dead couple brought a suit against the town claiming wrongful eviction, demanding exorbitant damages that, if granted, would've wiped out an entire generation of warm boys and girls.

In the meanwhile, Bernard spent everyone of his days off with his pet out in the backyard of his cottage turning it into a proper garden, a glorious little patch of green where Gaiety could frolic amongst the fruits, veggies and flowers. More likely it would not frolic, but rather do whatever it was it did in lieu of frolicking, and at least now it would be doing it in a more pleasant environment.

"I've been promising to do this for you for quite some time now, and if you can't do for the ones you love, well then what's the point of it all?" He stopped hoeing and leaned on the handle, gazing with his first smile in weeks at the little toady where it rested on the ground watching with great apathy a blue-winged gentlemanbug sitting on the leaf of a grape vine winding in through the neighbor's side of the fence. Gentlemanbugs are considered a juicy treat by most reptiles and amphibians, but the toady wouldn't even deign to lean forward enough to lick it up. "You're a lazy lump on a log, my friend, but I'm glad you're here with me and we're doing this together." Bernard went back to hoeing a row, while Gaiety simpered at the later sentiment.

A flutter of wings and a prolonged squawk preceded a parrot as it perched precariously on the wobbly gatepost.

"Come visit Kennari! Come visit Kennari," it repeated until Bernard fed the bird and let it recoup enough to recall the full message. Apparently Miss Kennari now lived quite a distance away, but she invited him to visit whenever he was free. A letter with a fuller explanation arrived a week later. It explained about her new job, which must have paid well, because also in the envelope was one ticket for a ferryboat ride to March Fjord.

THE END

145